Also by Megan Heissner

Two Steps Forward, Ten Steps Back
Not Quite Broken, Not Quite Perfect

This book is dedicated to my editor, my director, my fellow actor: Caleb.

8 January 1994

Chapter 1

William was staring deep into his book while he played with Frances' hair. Her freckled face was buried in his chest as she slept peacefully.

"How's the reading going?" a voice asked.

Looking up, William raised an eyebrow as he realized how close Roger's face was to his own. "Have you ever heard of perthonal thpathe?"

"No. What are you reading?" Roger asked again.

William held up the book and tapped the very visible cover. *Nebulans: Heritage and Culture.*

"That's your book, isn't it?" Roger yelled across the room.

In the kitchen, Philip and Isabel were talking while leaning against the island counter. Philip diverted his attention to Roger. "What?" he asked before shaking his head, "No, it's one of my mom's."

The five were all gathered in Isabel's house. She had invited everyone over a few hours prior. Although William had argued with Frances that he was busy reading, she still dragged him over. He had kept his crooked nose buried in his book the entire time.

"So, yeah. It's yours," Roger argued.

William slowly put his face back into his book.

It had been a bit of a hard last month. After William had been admitted into the hospital, he went into surgery, an event he did not remember too well and was glad not to remember too well.

He had teleported too much. *Aliens* had an energy they made in their appendix and used to activate their powers. The energy William had access to was less in comparison to most *aliens*, but William had still used far too much energy. So much energy that it would hurt any *alien*.

William had been right to suspect that the screws in his neck were *alien*. The screws were used for training *aliens* to restrict their use of energy and help prevent them from using too much and running into a problem.

Dr. Haming, Philip's mother, had been horrified to find the screws in his neck. She explained that she could not possibly understand why they were on him, especially if Kate had found him at ten months old with the screws already there. Not to mention, she had found him with two.

Although William had asked Dr. Haming if she could take them off, she had explained that it was almost impossible without the original remotes. The screws would each have had a remote with special access.

She offered to take them off manually, but she had warned that it could cause problems to his spine. Kate refused without giving it a second thought. At the time, William had been a little more than mad.

The energy that William was producing was killing him. Because the screws physically restrained how much energy he could access at any given time, his body had slowly begun to extract the energy from his appendix and store it in any cavity it could find. His heart, kidneys, lungs, liver, stomach, brain. Every cavity had filled up with energy.

NOT QUITE BROKEN, NOT QUITE PERFECT

He had experienced a heart attack on the operating table because the energy had overloaded his heart. He had almost died.

The hospital installed a fake, synthetic appendix in the hopes that his body might react positively to it. If his body was bent on extracting energy, there was the chance it might start placing it in the fake appendix instead of finding other places to store it.

It had been working for the most part which everyone seemed grateful for. Everyone. Personally, William found it unusual how much everybody seemed to care. Almost dying makes people care a lot, and William was annoyed with all of it.

Abilities started in *aliens* at *reckoning* age, which was the day an *alien* turned eighteen. Dr. Haming explained that the date Kate had picked as William's birthday was most likely inaccurate and pinpointed that he had probably turned eighteen the day his vision went haywire at school: November 18th.

Aliens could have bad reactions to *reckoning* since it was their first experience with abilities. Philip's mother further said it would be a transition, but William would slowly be able to use more of his powers, and she would continue to find ways to work around the screws.

William had become a little hesitant to use the powers. The near-death experience had made him slightly more cautious.

Currently, William had occasional checkups at the hospital where he was required to wear his 'AMALGAM' wristband.

Amalgam was a less degrading name for 'mixed blood.' William was part *nebulan*, the teleporting side of him, and part *archiec*, the fire side.

If he hated one thing more than being an *alien* it was being two different kinds of *aliens*. *Amalgams* were considered disgusting, lesser creatures in space culture. William could not care less what space thought, but he could try to care a little more when it came to human beings.

Frances loved him.

She did not care that he was an *alien*. In fact, she was trying to be supportive in any way she could. Mostly, she showed it through theories.

As of recently, her theories had revolved around several historic characters who she theorized were *aliens*. William found it comedic, and he appreciated every theory she made.

It had taken a bit of effort on her behalf, but Frances was the one to convince him to take up Philip's offer and read up on *alien* culture. Although William was wary, Frances was just the opposite. Anytime he read from any book, she asked him to read it aloud so she could hear about the wonders of the *alien* world.

At the present, William felt a little guilty reading while she was asleep. He figured he could always reread it, but it did not stop his shame.

"So what have you learned about *nebulan* heritage and culture?" Roger asked.

"What exactly are *nebulans*?" Isabel asked.

"*Aliens* who have the ability to move through space. A subspecies of *nebulans* are teleporters which is what Bill is," Philip cut in.

NOT QUITE BROKEN, NOT QUITE PERFECT

Philip had been enjoying the added attention Isabel had been giving him lately. Isabel was fascinated by *aliens*, and Philip was the *alien* expert.

"How many subspecies are there?" Isabel asked.

Philip opened his mouth before closing it. "I don't know. *Nebulans* aren't my species."

"Bill?" Isabel called.

"About twelve according to thith book," William explained.

"About twelve?" Roger repeated.

"A thub- thubth- thu-" William started.

"Subspecies?" Philip suggested.

"That," he replied, pointing at Philip, "It'th a theory that a new form of *nebulanth* are coming to form. They've adapted in a thertain way and are now conthidered a new thub- whatever."

"Cool! What does the *nebulan* world look like? Is it pretty?" she asked.

"The galacthy? No," William answered.

"It's a galaxy. How is it not pretty?" Roger asked, bewildered.

"Guardian-" Philip and William both started before stopping and exchanging a quick look.

"What?" Roger asked.

"Guardian Adonith dethtroyed the economy and now the *nebulanth* are all in debt bondage and thlavery," William explained.

"That's terrible," Isabel said.

"Yeah," Philip said, slowly nodding. He put his hand on Isabel's. She turned and looked at him and started to smile. At the sight of her smile, Philip started to get some color in his pale face as he began to blush.

"What? Why are you holding hands and smiling?" Roger groaned before turning his back to them and dropping on the recliner. "I'm curious. Is it upgrading or downgrading if I go from a third wheel to a fifth?"

"Downgrading," the other three replied.

Frances shifted in her sleep, and William held her a little tighter.

"When do I get a girlfriend?" Roger asked.

William pressed a kiss into Frances' hair. "It'th not that eathy-"

"I could always set you up with somebody," Isabel interrupted, "I'm a good matchmaker."

"When have you ever been a matchmaker?" a voice piped up.

Everyone turned to Frances who was attempting, through her grogginess, to push herself up from William's chest.

"Frank, you're gonna break my thternum," William murmured, as he winced in pain.

"Sorry," she whispered as she sat up.

"I got you two together," Isabel defended.

"You told him to take me to prom?" Frances asked quizzically.

William looked into his book and tried to focus on the words in front of him. According to the book, *nebulans* were a defensive race. They were often more in touch with their flight response.

Before reading about the *nebulans*, William had read about *archiecs*, who were considered one of the most aggressive races of all. William wondered why on earth a *nebulan*, a member of one of the timidest races, would ever have a child with an *archiec*. *Amalgams* were considered disgraceful, and the act of having a mixed race child could result in the death penalty.

His parents had obviously gone through a lot of trouble to bring him into the world.

"What a wathte of time," William muttered under his breath.

"Bill," Frances said, interrupting his thoughts.

"What?" William asked, snapping back into reality and lowering his book.

"He was all flustered, and I told him to ask you to prom and see your response," Isabel explained to Frances.

"Did you also tell him to kiss me so awkwardly that he would panic and accidentally cause both of us to fall into the school's indoor swimming pool?" Frances asked, as she turned to William.

With brows furrowed, William frowned. "Again, I'm thorry for that. Thintherely."

"It's okay. It was funny," she explained, before she pressed a kiss to William's nose.

"It wath not my fault-"

"It was Richard's?"

"It wath Rithard'th," he affirmed, before pointing to Isabel, "and it wath yourth too."

"I need this story now," Roger said, sitting up in his chair, "You pushed her into a pool?"

"Back off," William growled.

In the next second, the door opened. Lucas rushed in as fast as he could. "Isabel!"

"Hi!" His sister greeted before picking him up and into her arms.

Grace Saunders walked into the house. She was smiling, but her eyes betrayed that she was quite tired. The five-year-old often had that effect on people.

"Oh!" she exclaimed, seeing the five teens gathered in her house, "Hello, everyone. I hadn't expected anybody to come over. I would have cleaned up had I known."

"Don't worry. I did a full house clean," Isabel explained.

Of course, she had. Isabel, the planner and neat freak, was always busy doing something. William was not surprised.

Smiling, Grace kissed her granddaughter's cheek. "Thank you, sweetheart. I'll leave you kids alone. I'll be in my room so just yell if you need me, Isabel."

Excitedly, Lucas kicked his legs haphazardly. The tiny preschooler seemed thrilled to be hanging out with the seniors. "Put me down," he pleaded with Isabel.

"Okay, okay. Yeesh," Isabel groaned playfully.

She set him back on the ground, and Lucas moved to the middle of the living room in order to soak up all of the attention.

"You wanna watch cartoons?" Isabel suggested.

"That's for babies," he argued.

William chuckled before burying his face in Frances' hair as a means to stifle his laughter.

Scurrying onto the sofa, Lucas picked up the remote control and turned on the television. "I'm gonna watch the news like an adult," he asserted.

Roger tried to keep from smiling by putting both hands on his face.

The five-year-old flipped through the channels until he landed on a news channel and promptly sat down to watch.

"-we've got *demons* in Asia, and man-killing *crows* in North America!" a voice on the television rang out.

Slowly, William pulled his face away from Frances and stared at the screen.

"Hey, Lucas, maybe we should change the channel," Frances started.

"I want to watch! I'm old enough!" he yelled.

"This footage was taken in Mexico, approximately three hours ago. We would like to warn our audience that the footage they are about to see could be considered disturbing and to watch at their own discretion," the newscaster continued, before the show cut to a video.

"Lucas, give me the remote," Isabel said, as she approached her brother.

Holding the remote close to his chest, Lucas tried to stand up on the sofa and play keep-away "No!"

With brows furrowed, William watched the video.

"Lucas," Isabel pleaded.

Four large *crows* sat on top of a short building. They stared down at the crowd that was looking and pointing at them.

One *crow* opened its mouth and revealed a set of sharp teeth. It screamed a hideous call.

"What is that?" Roger whispered. William could just barely hear him over Isabel and Lucas' screaming match.

"*Kreshlings*," Philip whispered. His face was filled with a look of horror.

"I thought they were a defensive race," Frances mumbled, as she turned her head to William.

"They are," William affirmed.

From his readings, he knew that *kreshlings* were bird type *aliens*. They possessed large wings which they could grotesquely fold into their body.

However, this looked wrong. William was unsure why Philip was calling these things *kreshlings*, since *kreshlings* were part humanoid, and there was nothing humanoid about these creatures.

Then again, *archiecs* were not meant to look like *demons*.

The three other *crows* began to squawk and scream.

"Lucas!" Isabel yelled.

"Bill's on my side," Lucas yelled, hopping down from the couch and standing next to William, "Aren't you?"

It was sudden but in the next second, all four *crows* dove into the crowd. The people tried to disperse as quickly as they could, but the *crows* picked up a young girl who, in response, screamed at the top of her lungs.

As his brows rose, William clasped his large hand over Lucas' face and covered the child's eyes. William was not about to let the boy watch the *crows* as they pulled the girl limb from limb.

"Bill!" Lucas yelled, trying to pry the enormous hand away from his face.

"Lucath, thtop it!" William shouted while he kept his gaze trained on the television.

The crowd gathered around the bloody mess of what was left of the girl, while the *crows* flew back to their perch on the building's roof.

"What...?" Isabel faltered, putting her hand over her mouth in terror.

"What happened?" Frances asked, as she nervously turned her head from one person's general direction to another's.

"They killed a girl," Roger explained. His voice sounded hoarse, and William could assume that the video had left Roger's mouth dry.

"I think I'm gonna be sick," Isabel said, "They eat people?"

"No," Philip said, shaking his head in disbelief.

"What's going on?" Lucas yelled, still attempting to pull William's hand off. William was stern, and his hand was not going anywhere.

"Then why-" Isabel started.

Everyone, minus Lucas, turned their attention to Philip. They waited for an answer from the expert.

"I don't know," Philip whispered, hollowly.

Chapter 2

Thalassa was the victim, who cried on camera and lamented that her beautiful treaty had been stopped. She talked on television about how terrible it was that she had been criminalized by a false tape. The group's real and legitimate, claimed 'false,' tape.

As the *kreshlings* ravaged Mexico, Thalassa sent her condolences to those affected. She liked to remind the world that had her treaty not fallen through, she would have been able to use the military to protect everyone.

Thalassa had explained that the video taken in December was not credible and could not be authenticated. The public was slowly taking her words and being swayed to her side and now, there was a general hate for the man behind the video camera: William. No one knew it was William, but the media screamed about how he had maligned and slandered Thalassa's good name and that they hoped he felt shame for his actions.

He did not.

The *kreshlings* may have been new terrible news, but the *archiecs* were still just as terrible as any other news. Their attacks had spiked tenfold, and Earth was becoming more dangerous by the day.

The president of China had been found dead in his private quarters last week. Dead in a room that no one else had access to outside of himself and a few security personnel.

NOT QUITE BROKEN, NOT QUITE PERFECT

There was one way in and one way out, and the president was found burned to death in that room, while guards were stationed outside. The guards had no clue how anyone got inside, but they lost their lives over the ordeal.

William could only wonder if Thalassa was working with *nebulans* now. If someone had teleported inside.

The group was already certain that Thalassa was behind the *kreshlings* and if *nebulans* were involved, she was responsible for them too.

It made William furious. Everything did.

He had risked his life and the lives of those he cared about. In return, he had expected their hard work to pay off, and someone to kick Thalassa off the planet.

Thalassa had spun the entire story to make herself the victim, and William was mad. She could not get away with this.

From all that William had read about Thalassa, it appeared to be that she got away with everything, starting when she was a 'guardian-in-training.'

The process of becoming a guardian was hard. First, the guardian in power would need to handpick an ambassador, the 'guardian-in-training.' When the guardian would die, the ambassador would move up the rank and go through a coronation. In coronation, the ambassador's abilities would be enhanced, and they would be proclaimed a guardian of their race.

It was a popular belief that if a guardian conceived a child after the coronation, the child might be born with more powerful and dangerous abilities. Because of this belief, there was a law stating that guardians must partake in chastity. The law did not bar ambassadors from having children but once an ambassador became a guardian, the law took effect.

However, the guardians seemed to disregard the law entirely as laws apparently did not apply to them. The guardians did as they pleased and so did Thalassa.

A rumor had it that Thalassa had conceived a child after her coronation: a son named Llacheu. Considering all William had managed to see on Thalassa's ship, it was more than a rumor.

The picture on the ship projected by the orb mentioned a Llacheu and *reckoning*. It seemed like the *demon* child was of age and had dangerous powers to unleash.

Somewhere, Thalassa had a child. William was not sure what she meant to do with Llacheu but knowing her, she could only have bad intentions for Earth.

There was an issue that was more important, however. According to galactic law, which William had been reading up on a lot, guardians were prohibited from crossing into the Milky Way Galaxy. Earth, or Haven as *aliens* liked to refer to it, was off-limits to the guardians.

The planet had received the name Haven mostly because *aliens* often fled to the planet as refugees. It was also called Haven because the planet used to be inhabited by a species called *havenesks*.

The *havenesks* were a race of *aliens* who were once part of the guardianship. They decided several thousand years ago that they could not in good conscience remain in the guardian alliance and broke away. However, before leaving they made an agreement that no guardians would set foot in the Haven galaxy.

NOT QUITE BROKEN, NOT QUITE PERFECT

The race was considered to have gone extinct, but William had his own theory about the matter. Personally, he thought that the *havenesks* might have adapted and lost their abilities. The species originally had powers to temporarily expand bone and cartilage as well as increase hair growth. To William, they sounded like large mammals.

It also sounded eerily like the students in the test tubes. Animals.

Thalassa was not only breaking intergalactic law by trespassing on Earth but also she was conducting human experimentation on the inhabitants of Earth.

It was sickening. It was more than sickening.

William stared into his locker before sighing and resting his head inside.

Everyone in the school hall was either yelling about Thalassa or the *kreshlings* or the *archiecs*. The world felt like nothing more than a broken record, and it had William tired.

"I just need to grab my Calculus book real quick," a voice said, "Oh hey!"

Pulling his head out of the locker, William turned to see Isabel with Philip and Roger behind her. "Hi."

"What are you doing?" she asked with a smile as she unlocked the locker door.

"I have no clue," he explained before pulling out his Biology textbook, slamming the locker door shut, and reattaching his lock.

"Well, I'm off. Bye, Philip," Isabel said before pressing a kiss to Philip's lips.

William grimaced, before his ever-darting eyes tried to find something else to look at. He thoughtlessly scratched at his splint.

Quickly, she pulled away from the kiss. "Oh! I signed up Lucas for this group called the 'Little Adventurers,' and I also signed you up to be a helper," Isabel explained to Philip.

Philip's eyes widened, but he nodded. "Oh, okay."

William blinked and stared ahead at the lockers opposite of him.

"It'll be every Thursday afternoon, and it's just once a week," she said.

"Okay. It sounds good," Philip replied.

"I'm free," William mouthed to himself.

He turned to see Roger who was staring at him. Evidently confused, Roger began to mouth things to William and before long, the two were engaged in a quiet shouting match.

"Thank you so much, and- what on earth are you two doing?" Isabel yelled, as she took notice of Roger and William.

"You have thigned me up to do thingth for yearth," William said, "and now, it ithn't me. It'th Philip."

Philip looked a tad nervous, but Isabel was upset. "Hey!" she cried.

"I'm free," William said to the ceiling.

"You don't have to be so dramatic," Isabel said with a frown.

"Really? Seriously- that's where your mind goes?" Roger asked.

William grinned goofily. "Thith ith the betht day of my life." He started to walk past Philip before turning to him. "Thank you."

"You're welcome?" Philip replied hesitantly.

NOT QUITE BROKEN, NOT QUITE PERFECT

"Are we all still meeting up for dinner tonight?" Roger yelled.

Turning around, William walked backward with a smirk on his face. "Yeth, obviouthly. Why even athk?"

11 January 1994

Chapter 3

"You know, if you really want to, I could sign you up with Philip-" Isabel started.

"Hard path," William replied.

The two were walking together to Blockbuster, and Isabel had been talking nonstop about how thrilled she was for Philip and Lucas to spend more time together.

William pushed the front door of the Blockbuster open and walked inside with Isabel following close behind. The darting eyes scanned the store before William furrowed his brows.

"Where ith Jordan?" he asked.

"Bogey, no!" a voice shouted.

The two turned to their right to see a chow chow bounding towards them.

"Wh-" William began before the rather large puppy jumped on him and pushed him to the ground.

"Bad dog!" Jordan yelled, as he came barreling over, "Off!"

"I thought you had a samoyed," Isabel said, looking at the chow chow.

Just as William managed to prop himself up, another dog tackled him back down. It was the samoyed.

"Blazer! Bad girl! No," Jordan chided, desperately trying to pull the forty pound dog off of William.

"When did you get permithion to bring your dogth to work?" William yelled.

"I didn't so shush," Jordan replied, as he held his large samoyed close to his chest.

"You can't bring them here," William said on the ground, as he pointed at Blazer.

Evidently enjoying all of the attention, Blazer panted happily. Her tail wagged as she looked up at her owner and tried to lick his face.

"What's your name, baby?" Isabel asked, all while scratching the chow chow lovingly behind the ears.

"That's Bogey. I got him for Christmas, and he is the dumbest dog to ever live," Jordan explained.

"Your parenth got another dog?" William asked.

"No, but I wouldn't put it past them. My mom has almost adopted three cats this month alone," Jordan reflected.

"It'th only the eleventh of January."

Jordan blinked. "Yeah. This month alone. Three cats."

"Why is he dumb?" Isabel asked, as she scooped Bogey into her arms.

"Because he has half a brain and likes to do stupid things like jump out of moving cars," Jordan explained.

"The dog wath made for you," William grumbled.

Blazer, the samoyed, growled and like the feral animal he was, William growled in reply.

"Okay. I've finished the schedule-" Dave started, as he emerged from the breakroom, "Bill, why are you on the floor?"

"Athk Bogey," William grunted, as he finally got to his feet.

Dave looked to Jordan and Isabel who were each holding a dog. "Jordan, I have no problem with Blazer, but who is the chow chow?"

"His name is Bogey, and his IQ is in the negatives," Jordan explained, "He'll be good though. Blazer has been teaching him. Watch."

Jordan set Blazer down before taking Bogey from Isabel's arms and setting him down next to the samoyed. "Blazer, sit," Jordan commanded.

Just like the good girl she was, Blazer sat, wagging her tail excitedly. Bogey watched her before he rolled onto his back and happily wriggled his little chow chow body around.

Dave stared at the two dogs for a moment before turning to Jordan. "Just this once."

"Great! If anything goes wrong, it was all Bill's idea," Jordan deflected.

"I will murder you," William hissed.

Near closing time, William was reshelving videos with Bogey who was watching William very closely. The happy chow chow had been trailing him all night.

"Welcome to Block- hey!" Isabel exclaimed.

William turned to look at the entrance. It was Philip and Roger.

Looking around the Blockbuster, Roger turned to William, and he waved. Confused, William waved back.

William turned his attention to Philip and carefully studied Philip's face.

Philip's face was grave and accompanied by a hardened look. It was certainly a change in comparison to his usual quiet and soft demeanor.

While Isabel, Philip, and Roger were talking by the counter, William watched Roger bite down into his thumb.

NOT QUITE BROKEN, NOT QUITE PERFECT

The three passed glances amongst each other before collectively turning to William. In response, William raised an eyebrow.

Although he expected them to approach him or call him over, the three continued to talk among themselves in hushed tones.

William looked down at Bogey. "How muth you wanna bet they're talking about me?"

Bogey wagged his tail and began to bark erratically.

"Bill!" Isabel called.

With a sigh, William set down his box of videos on the floor and walked over to the others. Enthusiastically, Bogey jumped along.

"We need to talk after you two finish your shift," Philip explained.

"Really?" William asked, unfazed.

"Nothing bad," Roger reassured him.

"Your entire body language thayth otherwithe."

After closing the store and helping Jordan get his dogs inside his car, the four gathered at the front of the Blockbuster.

"We want you to break back into Thalassa's ship," Philip started.

William stuffed his hands into his pockets as his brows furrowed in displeasure. "Why?"

"Thalassa is playing victim on television while the *kreshlings* and *archiecs* are destroying everything," Philip explained, "We need to figure out her next move."

"He thought it'd be good to use the inside man," Isabel continued, as she nudged William with her shoulder, "Plus, you've been doing better since your accident, and this might be a good time to get back into teleporting."

"What are your thoughth?" William asked, looking to Roger.

Roger, who had been staring at the ground for a while, finally bothered to look up. "I'm a stand-in for the voice of reason here."

"Alright. Lay it on me."

"You were hospitalized last time you teleported," Roger reminded, bleakly.

"He's been cleared," Philip interjected.

"Bill," Isabel piped up, "In the end, it's your choice but-"

"But you would like to thway me to your thide, right?" William finished.

Isabel opened her mouth before clamping it shut. She knew the truth.

"I'll think about it," William said.

"You'll what?" The three asked.

"That'th not a yeth or a no. That'th an 'I'll thleep on it,'" William explained.

"Bill, we don't know how much time we have left before Thalassa does something of severe consequence-" Philip started.

"Everything the'th done hath been of thevere conthequenthe," William replied.

"You're actually considering this?" Roger yelled over William.

"You know it's the right thing-" Isabel interrupted.

"Alright- everybody, thut up!" William yelled.

Everyone fell silent.

"Thith ith my dethithion and mine alone. Whatever I conthider right will be right, and there will be no argumenth becauthe I'll be right," he explained.

The three exchanged nervous glances, but no one said anything.

They knew he was right.

~§~

The room was dark.

Rubbing his face, William stood up. He made his way out of his room and went downstairs in search of something to eat as if eating might solve his problems.

He could not sleep and although he was exhausted, it seemed exhaustion had nothing to do with the ability to sleep. As his head swarmed, he scratched at his beard and mole.

If he teleported, he could put himself in danger. He could be in terrible pain. If he did not, he would be risking the lives of everyone else. No one would be able to prepare for Thalassa's plot, and he would not be able to protect anyone.

He knew what he was supposed to do, and he knew what the right move was; however, the idea of being in that horrible frame-shaking, agonizing pain conflicted with him.

So there he was: leaning against the kitchen counter, holding a bag of bread, and stuffing a slice of bread in his mouth. As William stared up at the ceiling, he wondered if the kitchen ceiling might have the answers that the bedroom ceiling did not.

"Down here," a voice whispered.

Slowly, William looked down at the kitchen island to see Bear, Frances' Maine Coon, staring at him. The black cat's eyes were glowing a bright orange and each eye was beaming a ray of orange light.

William furrowed his brows as he set down the bread bag. "What do you want?"

"You need to see her."

"'Her' who?"

"Thalassa."

"What?"

"Quick. Quick!" The cat's eyes widened, pouring out more orange light.

William gripped the counter behind him. His brows rose as he watched the cat.

The cat's voice was growing in volume. "Quick!" it screeched.

"I don't even know where the ith!" William yelled.

"Quick!"

As he tried to think of where Thalassa could be, William thought of the balcony that overlooked Thalassa's study. He focused on the scene and in mere seconds, the kitchen and the cat faded away, and William was back in the cold, steely ship.

He was relieved to be away from the cat, but he was not so relieved to be back on Thalassa's ship.

Looking over the balcony, William found the study to be empty. However, he could hear voices nearby.

"Nagelfar!" Thalassa shrieked.

"I only want to see what they're like-" a male voice began.

"You may have power to station your *kreshlings* in Haven, but you have no power to tamper with my tests!" she yelled.

They were in the other room.

William turned around and walked down the hall until he came to the testing room with the four large tubes.

Facing away from him, Thalassa and a man with large wings were looking at one of the college students who was suspended in the tube. William immediately identified the man as one of the guardians from the portrait. He had long greasy, curly black hair and was wearing a black tabard.

"Thalassa, I am really worried. I think we need to go back and see the rest of the committee. We have no idea what Adonis might reveal. If he says anything, we will both-" the man started.

"Adonis is a coward. He is not about to say a thing against me," Thalassa replied.

With the weight of translating off of his shoulders, William merely stood there and listened.

Although each *alien* race had its own language, the *alien* common tongue was a certain variation of English. When William had first read that the common tongue was English, he had been relieved. That was a language he knew well and good and better than French.

Nagelfar continued to mess with the tube until the water began to drain, and Thalassa's yelling scared him off.

The student inside of the tube was a girl with chin length black hair and a very small, wiry frame. William wondered if the girl was naturally that small or if this was a result of Thalassa's inhumane experimentation.

When the water drained, however, the girl did not react. She barely moved.

"Is it-" Nagelfar started, appearing scared.

"This one did not take to the tests like the others," Thalassa explained before pressing a button and letting the tube fill back up with water.

"Where did you find these?" Nagelfar asked slowly, as he cautiously and nervously turned around the room to look at the other test subjects.

William backed up, trying to remain out of sight in case Nagelfar looked up at the balcony. William did not like Nagelfar referring to human beings as 'these.' 'These' were people who had been stolen from their families.

"They tried to sneak in while I was giving a speech in China. Their actions were their own undoing," Thalassa said plainly.

William looked out and as his eyes swept over the students afloat in their tanks, he became furious. Under different circumstances, it could have been him, Frances, Isabel, Philip, and Roger in those tubes. William was angry just imagining the scene.

"How long did it take the serum to start working?" Nagelfar asked.

"Well, the first batch took a week for them to take to. The second only took a few days," Thalassa trailed off. She picked up a vial and held it up, admiring its gleam. Or admiring her own handiwork. "I think my scientists have it down to two minutes."

"Two minutes?" Nagelfar asked in astonishment.

William furrowed his brows as he listened and after a moment, he noticed his mouth was slightly ajar.

As Thalassa approached Nagelfar, she held the vial close to his face. "You know, my scientists pump the serum into these things' stomachs because they simply cannot drink and eat in an unconscious state. But you can drink this. What might happen, Nagelfar?"

Nagelfar looked panicked as he tried to back away. "The serum is for *havenesks*. It cannot work on me," he blubbered.

"It absolutely can," Thalassa replied, "Think of the possibilities, Nagelfar."

"You are wanting to make *amalgams*?"

For as far away as William was, he could see Thalassa's eyes widen before she took a step back and hurled the vial as hard as she could at Nagelfar.

Nagelfar ducked, and the vial smashed against the wall behind him.

"How dare you-" Thalassa started.

"I simply do not understand. That is all. I am trying to make sense-" Nagelfar tried to explain.

"I am not making *amalgams*, Nagelfar! I am making things right. A *mutation* has no claim to life, and I have the power to give them whatever claim I please," Thalassa yelled.

William started to back up. He knew he needed to leave.

"Le garçon," a voice whispered.

As he turned around, William found himself staring at Ophelia. Her black hair was pulled up in its high ponytail, and she was staring at him with wide eyes.

"Le garçon!" Ophelia yelled. She hurriedly pushed past William and leaned over the balcony to continue her yelling. "Thalassa! Le garçon! Llacheu!"

William could just barely see past Ophelia as he was pushed up against the wall in an attempt to remain out of sight. He watched as Thalassa turned around and pulled some type of gun from her belt before firing. A laser blasted through Ophelia's face before she fell over the balcony.

"Thalassa!" Nagelfar screamed.

"Anyone who speaks that name is going to receive the same fate. I will not tolerate that name in my presence!" Thalassa yelled.

She put her wrist to her mouth before speaking into her bracelet. "Fouillez le navire."

'Search vessel.'

William had to get out. As he braced himself, he imagined the house's kitchen, and the scene came alive.

He was safe.

His eyes focused, and he noticed Bear still staring at him with his beaming orange eyes.

"What did he see? What did he see?" Bear asked, while a horrifying smile overwhelmed his face. He was not talking anywhere as fast or as urgently, and his head tilted from side to side in a demonstration of curiosity.

Processing Ophelia's death, William fell to the floor while tightly gripping onto the kitchen counter. Thalassa had been willing to sacrifice her own army; however, William had never considered that she would go as far as to sacrifice her own ambassador.

If those lives mattered so little, William could not even begin to consider how little the lives of the inhabitants of Earth mattered to Thalassa. They did not matter at all.

"Scared?" Bear whispered.

William tried to glare up at the cat, but he felt his glare falter. His face was still and every muscle in his body had seemed to lock up. He tried to pull himself back to his feet, but it was no use.

There was no line Thalassa was not willing to cross. There was nothing she was not willing to do. The ambassador was dead, and Earth would be too soon. And it would die at Thalassa's hands if William did not do something and fast.

[REDACTED]
[REDACTED]

Thalassa drilled her fingers against her desk.

While Layton pulled at his braided beard, Nagelfar stood nervously and stared at Thalassa. Layton had arrived only a few hours earlier and was less than pleased.

It was within seconds that the door to the study burst open violently.

"You killed Ophelia!" Adonis boomed, as he and Cenred walked into the room.

"It was a tragic accident," Thalassa muttered.

"No, it was not! You shot her!" Adonis yelled before approaching the opposite side of the desk.

Cenred's eyes were small, but they narrowed even further as he glared at Layton and Nagelfar. Nagelfar began to tremble and cower, and Layton started to look anxious himself.

"Now, how would you know something like that?" Thalassa asked, as she moved closer to Adonis' face.

"I-" he started, beginning to back up. He looked impeccably flustered.

"You hacked into my security cameras," she hissed.

Adonis stuttered awkwardly.

Nagelfar puffed up his chest and frowned. "Listen here, Adonis-"

"Sit down," Cenred commanded in a rumbly growl.

Nagelfar immediately did as he was told.

"You killed her for saying Lla-" Adonis began.

NOT QUITE BROKEN, NOT QUITE PERFECT

Thalassa screamed before taking a book from her bookshelf and setting it on fire. She threw it in Adonis' direction. The flaming book narrowly missed his head as he ducked.

"I will not have that name spoken in my presence!" Thalassa yelled.

"Are you mad?" Adonis squeaked.

"Hold your ground, Adonis," Cenred instructed.

"I cannot believe you are backing a coward," Layton spat.

"I would love to say I cannot believe you are a traitor to your own kind, but it is very believable," Cenred roared.

Layton appeared furious, but he looked away. They both knew the truth.

"Quiet!" Thalassa shrieked, "Adonis, if that is all you have to say-"

"It's not," Cenred retorted.

"Should you not be tending to your wife?" Thalassa asked.

"I am not about to stand aside and play house while you destroy everything."

"Pity. Tell the children I say hello."

Cenred snarled.

"You have gone too far," Adonis warned.

"And I am to be under the presumption that you intend to stop me?" Thalassa asked.

Desperate, Adonis stared at Thalassa with a hurt expression and weak eyes. "This is not what Caracy wanted for you or anyone else-"

"You will not speak on his behalf when you know nothing!" Thalassa screamed.

"You have blinded yourself!" Adonis yelled.

"Out!"

"This needs to stop!"

"The only way I will stop is in war!"

All four men froze.

"Are you declaring war on the *nebulans*?" Cenred asked.

"No," Thalassa said simply, as she tried to compose herself, "I am saying that if Adonis has a problem with my dealings, he may declare war on the *archiecs*."

The room was silent. Adonis looked down at the floor as if searching for some kind of answer.

"I will have my guards escort you off the ship," she started.

"I am not finished," Adonis said, clenching his fists tightly.

"I am," Thalassa replied.

"You're not going to hurt my family," he asserted.

Thalassa's eyes narrowed at him.

"Please..." Adonis pleaded.

With a wicked smile, Thalassa pulled a book from her bookcase and opened it to reveal that the inside was hollow. Within the hollow book were two remotes. Pulling them out gently, Thalassa slowly ascended the spiral staircase to Adonis' left before she pressed a button on each remote. She then threw the remotes to the floor and crushed them underfoot.

"No!" Adonis yelled.

Cenred grabbed hold of Adonis and held him back, as Adonis screamed and shouted.

"I declare war!" Adonis shouted.

The large *recquad* tried to put his hand over his friend's mouth. "Adonis!" Cenred growled.

"The *nebulan* army is nowhere near fit enough to declare war," Thalassa said.

"Cenred, help," Adonis begged.

NOT QUITE BROKEN, NOT QUITE PERFECT

"I am not about to send my army to fight on foreign land," Cenred explained.

"No one will stand for this," Adonis argued, as he turned back to Thalassa, "When people discover what you are doing-"

"Who is going to stop me? Nagelfar? Layton? No. Sadbh? Maybe, with Cenred's manipulation," Thalassa considered.

"I have never manipulated Sadbh once," Cenred growled.

"But she's still a biased party."

Slowly, Cenred started to release his grip around Adonis, but Adonis tore himself away before turning to Layton and Nagelfar. "Why would you help her?" Adonis screeched.

"Thalassa actually treats us with respect, something the other guardians have never done," Layton quipped.

"Layton, you pompous-" Cenred started.

"An alliance with Thalassa serves our galaxies well," Nagelfar explained, as he stood up.

"For how long?" Adonis cried, "She's taking over Haven! How long until she takes over *Kwanestry* or *Quod*? How long until it is *Neblimsh* and *Resuvas* and *Lifere*?"

Nagelfar folded his arms and glared at Adonis, while Layton remained looking away at a wall. Turning to Thalassa, Adonis saw how she sneered.

"Al..." he started. He stared up at her behind his spectacles as a weak man.

"Leave," Thalassa demanded.

"This is hardly over," Cenred said, as he pulled on Adonis' shoulder.

"I think it is," Thalassa replied.

The two men left and slowly Layton and Nagelfar turned to Thalassa. She looked at them from the balcony.

"I want the *kreshlings* to infect all of Mexico before moving up to the United States. Layton, deploy the *quiznics* in Venezuela, but also station some on the East coast of the United States," Thalassa commanded.

The two nodded before leaving her presence.

Thalassa looked down at her feet and stared at the broken pieces of the remotes. She put on a look of disgust before walking away.

Chapter 5

William stared down into his bowl of cereal. He had not managed to sleep at all the prior night, and he felt both exhausted and on edge. At that moment, adrenaline pumped through his body and sped up his heart, but his head screamed in pain and pleaded with him for sleep.

"William?" Kate called.

He barely heard her. She was sitting down in the living room and looking at him while he stood in the kitchen. Her words were not making it into his empty head. He was more focused on the sound of the rain outside than anything.

As William's eyes closed, he slowly began to nod off.

"William!" Kate yelled. The plump woman stood up and quickly moved into the kitchen. She grabbed hold of William's cereal bowl before he could have the chance to drop it on the floor.

Opening his eyes, William took in a deep breath as he tried to wake himself back up. "I'm thorry," he apologized.

"Sweetheart, what is going on?" his mother asked.

He shook his head. "It'th nothing," he lied before adjusting his baseball cap a little lower over his eyes.

Although William was not the biggest fan of lying, lying was a far better alternative than telling Kate the truth. The truth would not bring anything good. If he told her that he had teleported and seen Thalassa, he would throw her into a panic, and she did not need that.

"Please talk to me," she pleaded.

Slowly, William raised his head until he could see the green eyes behind those circular glasses. Her green eyes locked with his brown, but William immediately broke the lock as he looked for anything else to focus on.

"I know… I know we're nowhere near as close as we used to be," Kate started.

Confused, William furrowed his brows and looked at his adoptive mother. "What?"

"We haven't talked much about what happened in New York or about you being an *alien* or… about anything, really," Kate explained.

William was silent as he stared at the floor. "Do you want me to leave?" he asked.

"What- no!" She yelled. Kate grabbed his face with both of her hands. "William, no."

"You didn't thign up for an *alien* kid. I don't blame you if you hate me or you're dithguthted by me-"

"I am nothing of the kind. I did sign up for an *alien* kid, and I love you, and I am by no means disgusted by you," she argued.

William raised a brow. "What?"

"I love you," she reiterated.

"No- what do you mean you did thign up for an *alien* kid?" he asked.

Opening her mouth, Kate started to say something before clamping her mouth shut and pulling her hand back. "Well, I-"

"You knew?" William asked.

As she nervously bit down on her bottom lip, Kate slowly nodded.

"Why- why did you never-" he started.

"I don't know," she confessed, "I didn't know how you might react. I was worried you might feel hurt or get mad or something."

Tiredly, William rubbed his eyes with his hands.

"I'm so sorry. Please forgive me," Kate pleaded.

"I forgive you," William said, "I jutht don't get it. You kept me for tho long, and I can't underthtand why-"

"I kept you because you needed a family," she said, "And I wanted to be that family for you."

"You did it to be a 'Good Thamaritan?'" he asked.

"I did it for more than just that. I did it because I didn't want to see you go to people who didn't know what to do with you. I felt like I might have known what to do and every time I visited the hospital, I was scared I would find that you had been adopted by someone else."

"The part where you wathed me in the hothpital for dayth wath true?"

A shy smile found its way to Kate's face, and she eagerly nodded as she leaned back on the island counter. "Of course," she answered. She did not seem to know what to do with her hands but decided it would be best to fold her arms across her chest.

"You knew from then?" William asked.

"I knew before then. I mean, most of the original story was true," Kate reflected.

"The first part was, at least. I was driving down the road and having a bad day. And this little spaceship flew past the truck and almost hit me before crashing into the side of the road.

"I got out of the truck and just stood there, shaking. And I approached the space pod thing, and it opened, and I jumped away and screamed. And inside was a baby. It was all scared and looking all over the place and just getting more panicked by the second. And I realized that the poor thing was just as scared as me if not more.

"So, I hesitantly picked up the baby. And you were all spooked, but you were trying your best not to cry," Kate said as she looked at William.

William stared at her.

"I put you in the truck's passenger seat and with a lot of effort, I managed to get the space pod into the truck and cover it with the emergency sheets and blankets I keep in the back. The whole drive, I kept one eye on the road and one eye on you. And I drove to the scrapyard, and I dismantled the pod with a hammer and basically smashed it to bits.

"I possibly could have actually used the parts, but I'd seen one too many horror movies and was scared of something tracking the space pod and coming after you and killing me or kidnapping you. Maybe you were an *alien* child sent away for your protection. I had no clue."

"Unlikely, but I'm flattered," William said.

Kate allowed herself to smile a little brighter. "I still took you home and made a little makeshift playpen to hold you. I watched you vigilantly. I was too scared to sleep, but I was exhausted and eventually just passed out. And I woke up, and there you were, inches away from my face. You escaped the playpen and were simply sitting down right in front of me. Looking back, that playpen was definitely not my greatest creation, but I had tried at least.

"But again, you were directly in front of my face, and I just screamed in panic and terror. I summoned all of Timbers with my screaming fit. You know, there weren't many of us back then. Probably only twenty people or something like that. But everyone still barrelled over because of my screaming, and I had to explain to everybody that I had found you while driving home and was trying to take care of you.

"You know the rest: I took you to the hospital, and I visited the hospital everyday for a week to look into the nursery and just watch you. And eventually, a nurse asked me which baby was mine, and I had to admit that I had brought in the 'John Doe' and wanted to make sure he was alright. And she told me to consider adopting you.

"I was a little scared and a little nervous, but I had Isabel's grandparents to thank for all the playdates. I got to watch you play and roughhouse and grow up and now..."

She fell silent and scrunched up her face as she searched for the right words to say.

"You know I'm proud of you, right?" Kate asked, "I'm so proud of you, William, and I'm so proud to call myself your mom."

William let himself smile for a brief second until his face grew serious.

"Why did you never tell me?" he asked.

Silence flooded the kitchen.

Kate let out a slow and quiet breath through her pursed lips. "You have every right to be upset-"

"I'm not upthet. I jutht want to know," William explained.

Kate was quiet. "Do you remember when you were six, and I told you that you were adopted?"

William stared at the floor and nodded. "I lotht my mind."

His mother nodded as well. "You did. You wouldn't talk to me for hours, and you were so upset. It wasn't until later in the day that you were willing to say anything to me at all. You told me you still considered me to be your mother, and it was such a relief. I shouldn't have held something like that from so long ago against you, but I was so worried of what might happen if I told you that you were an *alien*."

With a sigh, William rubbed his face. "I get it." He screwed up his face. "I'm thorry I went to New York without telling you."

"I forgive you," she said. She smiled up at him, but her eyes widened in a panic. Looking up at the microwave clock, Kate cursed. "I'm gonna be late!" She yelled, "You are too. We're both gonna be late."

William's mind was beginning to grow muddled with thoughts. There was too much rushing around in his head. He was thinking of Kate's words, but he was also thinking of Ophelia. Fixed, his mind was replaying the moment Ophelia's body fell over the balcony railing.

The things Thalassa was willing to do to her own people were horrific. As he considered Thalassa's detestable acts, William's mind slipped into thinking of what Thalassa could do to Kate.

As Kate grabbed her hard hat, William scratched at his beard.

"I love you," she said.

"I love you too," he murmured.

"Hey, what if I picked up something for dinner tonight?" Kate suggested.

He nodded slowly, his eyes glued to the floor. "That thoundth good."

"William?" Kate called.

William looked up to his mother. "Yeah?"

"Are you sure you're alright?" she asked.

The liar was unsure how to answer the question. He could tell her the truth but that might worry her. He could lie to her but that might also worry her if he was not convincing enough. It was not like he would try to actually be convincing. Of course, he would not convince her.

Lying always seemed to be the only good option, however.

"Yeah. I'm good."

Chapter 6

Slowly, William opened his eyes and stared at the ceiling. The room was dark. Although he could not be sure, he assumed it was probably somewhere close to midnight. He could hear heavy rain pouring outside.

"Bill?" a voice whispered.

Looking up and to his right, William saw Frances sitting on the couch. They were both in the living room although he was lying on the floor.

William had been given the day off from work and since neither he nor Frances were busy, they decided they would watch a movie at his house which they had both fallen asleep to while watching.

"Why are you awake?" William asked.

"Why are you awake?" Frances questioned.

"I athked firtht."

"I'm your girlfriend."

As he propped himself up on his elbows, William nodded. "Fair enough."

"Why are you awake?" she repeated.

Yawning, William closed his eyes tightly. "I have no clue. Probably becauthe I knew I'd forgotten to take you back home. Your parenth are gonna kill me."

"I doubt they know I'm still here. My dad probably fell asleep at the office or went out with his own party while my mom went out with hers."

NOT QUITE BROKEN, NOT QUITE PERFECT

William wondered if Kate was still asleep. When he had picked up Frances, he had also picked Kate up from her work. She had immediately gone to bed. If she had woken back up, she most likely would have yelled at her son about being more mindful and taking Frances back. Since the event had yet to occur, William could assume she was still sleeping.

"Alright. Your turn. Why are you awake?" he asked again.

"I couldn't sleep."

"Well, that'th obviouth. Why can't you thleep?"

"I don't know," she mumbled. William heard a voice in the back of his head tell him that she was lying.

Slowly, William climbed to his feet. He reached out for Frances and as he sat down on the couch, he pulled her to him. He realized that she was trembling ever so slightly.

"Hey, it'th gonna be okay. It'll all be alright," he said, "Why don't you tell me thome theorieth?"

Frances rested her head against his chest. "Could we watch something on the television?" she whispered.

As William furrowed his brows, he nodded slowly. "We can do that." Pressing a kiss into her hair, William picked up the remote control and changed the channels until he landed on a cartoon. He was not about to listen to the news tonight.

They sat in silence for a few moments.

"Will you tell me a theory now?" William spoke up.

"I don't have any new theories, good or otherwise," she responded in a quiet voice.

"Thure you do," he encouraged.

Frances remained silent.

This was not unusual. William had no idea what her dreams were but every now and again, Frances would have a nightmare that completely shut her down. She might still tease a bit and try to pass over the topic, but it would eventually consume her to the point that she would barely be able to function throughout the day.

It seemed like this was one of those times.

William took her hand before bringing it close to his face and pressing a kiss to her thumb.

"I wath reading up on the thcrewth," he said, as he tried to start a conversation.

She did not respond.

With a long exhale, William continued. "They're called *nikolateth*, but I mean, they're jutht thcrewth. That'th what I've alwayth thought of them ath: the thcrewth in my neck."

Nothing.

"They're uh… they're put on *alienth* to limit the amount of power they can uthe. Dr. Haming thaid the had no idea why I had them but maybe I tapped into my energy and abilitieth early."

"At ten months old?" Frances finally said.

"It'th a bad theory," William said as he furrowed his brows.

"Well, no," she continued, "I mean, you understand it's used for training *aliens* how to use their power, and you used that information to assume you had the power earlier than others. And you'd mentioned before that you read something about how *amalgams* are considered dangerous and more powerful-"

"*Amalgamth* are killed the moment they're born if not thooner."

"Which means your parents obviously tried to hide you and keep you safe before their hands were forced, and they had to send you to Earth," Frances explained.

Deep in thought, William nodded. "But that thtill doethn't ecthplain the thcrewth."

"Maybe they did it to make you look cool."

William raised an eyebrow and turned to her, trying to restrain himself from smiling. She was grinning. She knew the idea was stupid, and she obviously thought herself pretty funny.

"Really?" he asked, stifling his smile to the best of his ability.

"Yeah. Maybe they sat down one day and thought 'you know what would be really cool?'" she started, as she began to laugh.

"'Inthtalling a training devithe that hath abtholutely no buthineth being anywhere near a ten month old into our ten month old,'" William finished.

"I'm sorry," she wheezed through laughter.

"You aren't, you liar," he said as he began to smile.

"It's not funny. Why am I even laughing?"

"Are you feeling better?"

"Yeah," she said with a nod, as her laughter began to die down.

They sat close together and listened to the cartoon.

"Would you do the voice?" she giggled.

"You've been athking that ever thinthe I brought up that Roger compared my voithe to *Garfield*."

"It's so similar."

"It'th the ecthact thame thing! I'm doing the voithe jutht by talking!"

She tried to shush him the best she could.

After a small while, Frances reached out her hand and delicately touched the back of his neck. "They do make you cool."

"Uh huh?" he replied, trying to keep light-hearted. It did not feel cool. It felt dangerous. Either his parents wanted to see him hurt by the screws or they wanted to keep others safe from him. He wanted to believe it was the former, but even believing that felt painful enough.

There was no good reason for those screws to have been placed in his neck. There could simply not be.

William watched Frances frown, while she ran her fingers up and down his neck. "I can't find them."

Taking her hand, William moved it a little higher. "There-" he started.

They were not there. William touched the back of his neck and tried to find the two screws. They were gone.

"They're not there," he whispered.

"What?" Frances asked, pulling her hand back.

"They're not there," he repeated, "Why..."

"Did they fall off?"

"They can't. They both have a thpethific remote that unlatheth them."

Frances' eyes just barely made contact with his own, as her face turned to a look of worry. "What does this mean?"

"Thomeone found the remoteth and uthed them," he explained, as his brows furrowed. He was rubbing the back of his neck. Hard. Hard enough, he assumed, that he would leave it red and sore.

"So, you're free? You're gonna be alright- Bill! You're no longer in danger!" Frances exclaimed, as she wrapped her arms around his neck, "Energy isn't going to build up in your organs anymore. You don't have to worry about coughing up blood or your heart stopping or-"

"Why now?" he asked.

"What?" she started.

"Why would they take them off now?" he asked, looking into her blind eyes, "Thith ithn't good, Frank."

Her eyes widened slowly as she let go of him and sat back down.

"Thith ithn't good," he repeated.

Chapter 7

William found his mind to be far from the screws the next day as he entered the chess room. In the back of the room, he could see Roger and Philip playing chess together.

A force from behind pushed William further into the room. As he turned around, he noticed it was Isabel who was shoving him.

"Morgan?" William asked.

"Hey," she said with an enormous smile, "Are we playing chess today?"

"Don't you have a club of your own you thould be attending?"

"We rescheduled to meet for Saturday since the president had a family emergency."

"Huh. Well, Roger and Philip theem to be getting along jutht fine by themthelveth, and I'd rather-"

"Bill, they're our friends! Don't you want to spend time with them?" she started.

"Do I have to?"

Looking up, Philip noticed William before waving shyly at him. As Roger watched Philip, Roger turned around to see William and waved enthusiastically with an enormous grin.

William sighed as he adjusted his baseball cap. "Well, I gueth I have no thoithe now."

"You're acting ridiculous," Isabel chided, "You like them."

"I motht thertainly do not," he argued.

"What are you standing around for?" Roger yelled across the room.

It took some less than gentle persuasion but after a few minutes, Isabel forcibly pulled William over to the desk. William sat down next to Roger and Philip and opposite Isabel, but it was only a moment before Roger yelled that he wanted to play against William, and Philip and William had to play musical chairs and switch seats.

William had wanted to play with other opponents, but he would have to settle for Roger. However, it only took a few minutes for William to learn that Roger had his own set of rules he liked to play by.

"So now, my pawn becomes a double pawn," Roger declared, trying to put one chess piece on top of the other.

"What?" William asked.

"That's how the game works," Roger explained.

"What? No, it doeth not."

"Sure it does!" Roger retorted, "And with the magic power of teleportation, my queen takes your king," Roger knocked over William's king. "Checkmate."

"That'th not how it workth."

"But it should! Think of how much cooler chess would be."

William turned to Philip. "Do thomething."

"Do what?" Philip asked.

"Anything."

"It seems legitimate to me," Isabel piped up, as she smiled teasingly at William.

Making eye contact with Isabel, William glared at her. As he continued in his glare, William took hold of the chessboard and lifted it up before all of the pieces slid into Roger's lap.

"Hey!" Roger exclaimed.

"Be careful with those boards!" the chess president yelled, "They cost more than you're worth alive."

William pulled out his wallet and slapped a ten dollar bill down on the table.

"Carry on," she said.

"Chelsea!" Roger hollered at her.

"I thought her name was Lexie," Philip piped up.

"What is her name?" Isabel asked.

William shrugged, giving Isabel a quizzical look. As if he would know.

"It's Lindsey, thank you," the president said as she applied another coat of nail polish onto her pinkie nail.

"You can't just dump chess pieces on me," Roger argued.

"I jutht did," William replied, unbothered.

"You're more of a stick in the mud than usual."

"I'd argue he's about the same," Isabel said.

"If you're not gonna play by the ruleth, I don't thee any point in playing at all," William explained.

"Just about nobody plays by the rules in the real world," Roger replied, trying to act philosophical.

"Alright, well, theth ain't the real world."

"It could be. You gotta learn to adapt," Roger picked up the pieces off of the floor and reset the board. "Let's practice without the usual rules."

"Let'th not," William groaned, as he folded his arms across his chest.

"This is actually hilarious to watch," Isabel said.

William turned to Roger who was trying to explain how chess 2.0 was to be played. Unamused, William tuned him out and sat there staring blankly. The only thing he was listening to was the white noise ringing in his ears.

He began to run figure eights around his neck when he remembered the missing screws.

"I teleported to Thalatha'th thip a few dayth ago," William spoke up. He probably had not needed to be so blunt.

Roger jerked his arms and spilled the chess pieces back onto the ground.

"You did?" Philip asked in a quiet voice.

"Really?" Isabel asked.

"Are you out of your mind?" Roger questioned in the quietest voice William had ever heard him speak in.

"Alright, calm down," William started.

"Is reason dead? Does nobody care about what I have to say?" Roger started to yell.

"Quiet down," William rebuked.

"Shouldn't we talk about this somewhere more private?" Philip asked.

"Thith theemth private enough what with Roger yelling," William said.

"I'm not yelling!" Roger shouted.

William turned to Philip. "Nagelfar wath there," he started.

"You mean like the guardian?" Philip whispered.

"No, I mean like the world clath magithian- yeth, I mean the guardian!" William hissed in a low voice.

"What is he doing on Haven?"

"Letting the *krethlingth* lothe. Thalatha ith letting him thtathion them on the planet."

"He needs her permission?"

"Theemth that way. Thalatha doethn't like Nagelfar mething with her teth on the thtudenth from Thina. It lookth like the only reathon they were her candidateth ith becauthe they thnuck onto her thip."

"What, like you did?" Roger asked.

William nodded with a low sigh. "Only they got caught."

"What is Thalassa doing to them?" Isabel asked.

"The'th made thome kind of therum," William explained.

"A serum?" Philip asked for confirmation.

"The wath prattling on about the therum taking two minuteth to take effect. I don't know what it meanth-"

"She's recreating *havenesks*," Philip whispered.

"What?" William asked.

"Th... there's theories in the *alien* community on Earth about what Thalassa might be doing. She started a project probably a decade ago or maybe more where she wanted to see if she could manipulate biology and anatomy and restore energy to *aliens* who couldn't make *energy* on their own or who couldn't use it."

"The'th thanging humanth into *havenethkth*?" William started.

"Possibly."

"Ith that what the'th done with the *archiecth* and *krethlingth*?" William asked.

Roger froze in the middle of putting the chess pieces back in place. Roger exchanged a look with Philip before they both turned to William.

"No, those are *reversions*," Philip explained.

"What are *reversions*?" Isabel asked.

NOT QUITE BROKEN, NOT QUITE PERFECT

"*Reversion* is a state of being. It's when an *alien* uses too much *filrin*, or energy as I know William calls it. Their mind and body change. They lose a lot of cognitive thought and usually shift in physical features until they look more... *alien*. That doesn't really sound right. Until they look more like what Earth media portrays *aliens* to look like."

William stared down at the desk as his brows furrowed in thought. "Then, why are the *archiecth*..."

Philip frowned. "That was the most confusing part when they came. These are mindess, irrational *aliens*. In *reversion*, priority number one is survival. It was awful seeing so many *reversions*, especially since they were somehow on Earth in an environment they had never seen or experienced. They have no idea how to survive."

"Did Thalatha plant them here?" William pressed.

"That's the general assumption in the community," Philip explained, "There is no way that so many *aliens* bent only on their own survival could have found a way to get off of *Archia* and onto Haven- or Earth."

"What normally happenth when an *alien* goeth into *reverthion*?"

"Usually, they're transported to a safe house. Like I said, *reversions* only try to survive and nothing else. They attack if they think their life could be in danger or if they perceive someone to be a threat. *Nikolates*, the screws in your neck, are used to teach *aliens* how to use their powers little by little without running the risk of *reverting*. And once they learn, they can know their limit and know how much energy is safe to use.

"It's not terribly uncommon for *aliens*, especially recently *reckoned aliens*, to enter into *reversion*. When that happens, they're put in a safe house. *Reversions* can last from one week to two. I think the longest recording was five weeks? Your body overheats from too much energy, and *reversion* is just the cooldown. You get stuck in the state depending on how much energy you used."

"Well, hold on," William said, straightening in his chair, "The *archiecth* in Athia have been like that for far longer than jutht five weekth. What are we coming up on?"

"Four months?" Roger suggested, hollowly.

Philip winced and looked down into his lap. "It's frightening for the humans on Earth but believe me... it's frightening for the *aliens* on Earth too."

William rubbed the back of his neck and tried to recall more from what he had heard that night. "Thalatha thaid thomething about curing *mutationth*."

Philip's entire face went blank before becoming confused and bewildered. "Is that what this is all about?"

"What?" William asked.

"Philip-" Roger started.

"Was that what she said?" Philip questioned.

"It wath thomething about giving them a claim to life," William said, trying to remember.

"They do have a claim to life!" Philip yelled, as he stood up.

The chess club fell silent.

William stood up and grabbed Philip by the arm before pulling him out of the room. Roger and Isabel followed close by, but Philip was in a rage.

"They do have a claim!" Philip continued to shout.

"Calm down," William hissed through gritted teeth.

The four stood outside by the lockers.

Philip was out of breath. His face had gained some color in his fury as he now looked a little pink instead of his usual pale and ghostly look.

"*Mutations* are *aliens* that can't access energy. They are considered to be low lives and usually live miserable and helpless lives if family members aren't willing to care for them," Philip explained in a quiet voice.

"The'th helping a populathion?" William asked, confused.

"No, she's not!" Philip yelled.

William shushed him, and Philip quieted down. "The guardians were the ones who decided that *mutations* had no claim to life," Philip explained, "And they still consider them to have no claim from what Thalassa apparently says. The *havenesks* considered all *aliens* to have worth. When they had children who did not have abilities, they still cared for them and after a hundred generations or so, no *havenesk* had abilities and that's why they're just humans now. And there's nothing wrong with that! But Thalassa has to come and change everything because she doesn't understand.

"Every human's life is worthless in her eyes. Don't you understand? All humans are *mutations* meaning that, as far as Thalassa cares, all humans have no claim to life."

William's brows rose.

"It's easy for her to kill us because we're nothing. We're either *mutations* or we're *alien* traitors who have deserted our planets. She might destroy all of Haven to give it her so-called purpose if that's what she feels is necessary," Philip said.

"Then why this war?" Isabel asked, "Why with the *archiec* attacks and the *kreshling* attacks?"

"To make us know we're weak," Roger spoke up softly.

William and Isabel turned around, and three sets of eyes were on Roger.

"She establishes that we can't stand against what's out there and when she infects us and we become 'better,' we'll have no choice but to thank her for what she's done," Roger said.

William frowned. It was plausible.

"Bill- Bill!" Philip yelped.

Raising an eyebrow, William looked to Philip before William looked to his own hand and noticed that the back of it was on fire. He put the flame out quickly.

"Thorry," William said hastily.

The room suddenly went dark. Straightening up, William tried to look around himself. A throbbing, coursing pain pulsed in his head, and William gritted his teeth in pain.

For a brief moment, he closed his eyes. When he opened them, he could see two bright, orange eyes staring at him in the dark room. A white, toothy smile emerged from underneath the eyes.

Just as abruptly as they had turned off, the lights turned back on. William blinked and tried to let his eyes adjust to the brightness.

"What..." he trailed off.

"What's wrong?" Roger asked in surprise.

"Why did the lighth go off?" William asked, as his gaze remained fixated at the place where the cat had been.

"They didn't..." Isabel whispered.

"Bill," Philip pleaded.

NOT QUITE BROKEN, NOT QUITE PERFECT

William noticed how tightly he was gripping Philip's sweatshirt and slowly released his hold.

He looked between the three before rubbing his face with his hands. He pushed his glasses up and as they fell back down to the end of his nose, he let his bleary eyes move from one blurry face to another. "I don't think I'm alright."

Crying.

The biggest crocodile tears William had ever seen in his life. It made the soup in his mouth taste disgusting. He was not about to stop eating but still. He was filled with a great uneasiness, and it made him tense. With each passing moment, he gripped his spoon just a little tighter.

His annoyance was great.

Thalassa was standing on a stage and crying on the news. It was quite the show, and William was having none of it.

The video was being broadcasted from Venezuela. Almost twelve hours ago, *quiznics* had begun sprouting *vines* in crop fields. The news station had no idea it was *quiznics*, but William knew that the destructive *vines* were being controlled by something.

In the last twelve hours, almost a third of all of Venezuela's crop fields had been sprouting these killer weeds. Landowners had reported their initial confusion at how active the *vines* were. However, the *vines* quickly turned vicious.

William had spent the last few hours watching different news stations play amatuer footage of *vines* shooting anywhere between ten to twenty feet into the air and grabbing hold of farm hands before dragging them back down into the Earth. The victim would scream and shout and then be swallowed whole by the ground. The unsettled dirt was the only sign that anything had occurred at all.

NOT QUITE BROKEN, NOT QUITE PERFECT

At first, the rest of the farm hands were trying to dig up their fallen friend and retrieve them. The only problem was that the *vines* took this as an invitation to pull more victims into the ground. The most recent videos showed farm hands running for their lives. It was everyone for themselves.

Recently, a plan had come into play to combat the *vines*. Landowners were employing the use of crop dusters which would fly over the fields and rain pesticides down on both *vines* and farm hands alike. It seemed to be working, and the *vines* were reacting negatively. It was working too well, though. The farm hands were reacting terribly to the pesticides as well.

No one seemed to care quite as much about that fact, however.

William dropped his spoon in his soup and set down the bowl before rubbing his face. Everything was a mess.

"Will you go to sleep?" a voice asked.

As he turned to his left, he could just barely see Kate standing on the stairs. "In a bit," he replied.

"It's my birthday. This is my birthday wish."

"I jutht need five minuteth," William protested.

"Please," she whispered.

"Two minuteth," he bargained.

"Two," she said sternly.

"Thank you," he said after her as she climbed back up the stairs.

Slowly, William let his head drop, and he sighed. As he raised his eyes, he watched Thalassa on the television. She was talking about sending aid to Venezuela, but she was uncertain how much help she could be.

She had helped enough.

Grabbing his bowl, William walked into the kitchen and threw it down into the sink. It was plastic. It was not like it would break. Still, he could have been gentler.

He slid the back door open and slammed it shut behind himself, while unleashing a slew of curses. He was furious. He was so furious he was shaking.

Once outside, William threw himself down into the dirt. He could hear the sound of cars rushing from the highway below.

Breathing. That was his one job: not to set on fire and to stay calm.

In the next moment, his face caught fire.

He had failed his job.

As he slowly tamed the flames, he looked up to see Bear peering down at him.

"What do you want?" William growled.

A third eye opened above the cat's two orange eyes.

Slowly, William opened his mouth. He was not entirely certain what to say. "Maybe don't do that," he suggested.

Several more eyes began to open all around the cat's face until it was full of eyes.

William got to his feet and entered the house while keeping his eyes on the cat's many eyes. Without breaking his line of sight, William grabbed the spray bottle and started shooting water at the cat's face.

The Maine Coon screamed and hissed before vanishing into the thin air.

As William ran a hand through his hair, he realized that he was completely drenched in sweat.

"Thtupid cat," he muttered.

NOT QUITE BROKEN, NOT QUITE PERFECT

The phone rang, and William turned around before throwing the spray bottle at it and knocking it off the wall. "It'th one in the morning! Don't call thith houthe!" he yelled.

The dial tone echoed in the house.

William breathed heavily before his darting eyes looked for something to distract himself with.

21 January 1994

Chapter 9

Sitting in the back of the library was William on the floor reading. Most students avoided the library, and those who dared to venture into it never got as far as the back.

Two books were lying face open in front of him: Thalassa's retelling of history and Thalassa's actual history. Earlier, William had pulled covers off some books at home to hide what he was reading. If someone happened to ask him what he was reading, he would show them a book with a history cover or a book with an astronomy cover. Or he could simply tell them to mind their own business and get lost. He was mostly relying on the latter.

Thalassa wrote of a fantasy love which blossomed between her and her personal bodyguard, a man named Caracy. Reportedly, it was true. Caracy had fallen madly in love with her and had devoted himself to her not just as a bodyguard but later as a husband.

Along the way, the *kreshling* ambassador at the time died by accident, and it left Thalassa devastated.

It was true. There was a *kreshling* ambassador named Venus who fell from her room's window. Her death was highly suspect, however.

Eventually, Thalassa and Caracy married, and Thalassa gave birth to a son. The couple named the child Gairbith. William was under the assumption that this might be Llacheu. Whether Llachcu was a pet name or a nickname, William had no clue.

NOT QUITE BROKEN, NOT QUITE PERFECT

Three years after Gairbith's birth, Thalassa's guardian died, and Thalassa became the new guardian. Most of the history recorded was mundane until approximately eight years after Thalassa had become guardian. She and the other five guardians tried to evacuate a dying planet and ready evacuation ships, when Caracy attempted to retrieve an unaccounted for child. He did not make it back to the ship, and the rest of the guardians decided to take off without him instead of risking the lives of the evacuees.

The planet died, and Caracy died along with it. Thalassa swore to never forgive her fellow guardians for leaving him on the planet.

However, as William read, it seemed like Thalassa was also responsible for her husband's death. All of the guardians had a role in updating and approving evacuation procedures and as the years went by, Thalassa spent less and less time carefully evaluating policies and instead pushed through many haphazard procedures. Those careless procedures were most likely responsible for the child being unaccounted for, and Caracy's selfless nature led him to his death.

Many years after Caracy's death, Gairbith reached the age of *reckoning* only for it to be discovered that he could not produce energy. He was a *mutation*. The discovery drove Gairbith to madness, and he blew up a building and himself along with it.

"Bill?" a voice spoke up.

William looked up.

It was Frances.

"Hey," he said as he reached up and carefully took her hand before pulling her down next to him.

"The librarian said there was a very stern looking student back here, and she thought I might know him," she explained with a smile.

"Oh ha ha," William said.

She began to laugh, and he brought her a little closer to himself. "What are you doing here?" he asked.

"I was about to ask you the same thing. Aren't you supposed to be at chess club?"

"They blew me off," William grumbled.

"Philip and Roger?" Frances asked.

"Yeah."

"Isn't that a good thing? Didn't you want to play with other members?" she reminded him. She reached out and rubbed her thumb over his cheek.

"I wathn't really in the mood," he lied.

"You like them," Frances whispered. A smile crossed her face, and she showed off her dimples.

"I don't."

"They interest you."

"They do not. What do you wanna do for dinner?" he asked, trying to change the subject.

Her smile was mischievous, and she pressed a kiss to his lips. He returned the kiss quickly.

"Pleathe," William said.

"I'll stop. I'm sorry. What are you doing here?"

"Thome Thalatha rethearth," he explained with a lot of difficulty.

"Tell me more," she said, scooting a little closer. She appeared serious yet intrigued, as she pushed her sunglasses into her hair.

Such pretty eyes.

"Well, according to Thalatha'th writingth, the had a thon named Gairbith. He didn't gain any abilitieth at *reckoning*, and it cauthed him to go inthane," William explained.

"*Reckoning* has to do strictly with abilities, right?" Frances asked for clarification.

"Right."

"And it happens at eighteen."

"Right again."

"Why were you late?"

"Kate thothe to make my birthday the day the adopted me whith wath the 12th of Theptember. In acthuality, my birthday ith the 18th of November."

"How does it feel to be younger?" Frances teased.

"I thtill beat you by a month," he replied before pressing a kiss to her thumb.

"Did he really go crazy or did she make it all up?" Frances asked, becoming more invested.

"Apparently, it'th true. He goeth inthane and then bombth a factory. In Thalatha'th book, the thayth that he dieth but eyewitneth accounth report that he wath arrethted. What happened after hith arretht ith pure thpeculathion. He fallth off the grid tho whether Thalatha killth him herthelf or not ith unknown."

"Do you think she'd kill her own child?" Frances asked.

William thought of Ophelia's body falling over the balcony's railing. "Yeah."

Frances was quiet for a while. "What else is there?" she spoke up.

"Well," William began hesitantly. He did not want to distress that freckled face anymore than he already had, but he continued. "Thalatha thtarth a project to thee if the can meth with biology and anatomy and rethtore energy to *alienth* who can't make or uthe it. The prattleth on about thimpler timeth and when the guardianth firtht fought for power. The talkth about how nithe it would be if only one guardian ruled them all, what it would be like to thtart freth, won't thtop running her mouth and yammering all over the plathe," William groaned, "and then it endth."

"There has to be more," Frances urged.

"There ithn't," he replied.

The two sat in silence. As William turned his head in her direction, he could see that she was deep in thought.

She scrunched up her round face.

"Isabel told me that you teleported to Thalassa's ship," Frances explained.

William raised an eyebrow. He had not realized that he had failed to mention his visit to Thalassa to Frances. "I'm thorry," he apologized.

"Why? Why did you go there?" she asked.

"We were in the dark. We needed anthwerth. Thpying theemed like the eathietht way to figure out what Thalatha'th necht thtep wath and what our necht thtep needed to be."

"What is our next step, Bill?"

William's brows furrowed as he stared at her. He had no idea how long he stared for. He was always used to his darting eyes moving everywhere but now they remained focused on all of those freckles and the eyes of a girl seeking answers that he could not provide.

"I don't know," he confessed.

Slowly, her face turned down, and she took his hand and intertwined her fingers with his.

As he frowned, William let out a long breath through his nostrils.

"Isabel was filling me in on the things you heard and the discussion you guys had last Friday at chess," she explained, "Thalassa wants to 'give us a purpose?'"

"The thaid the wanted to give uth a claim to life and the would give uth whithever one the wanted," he grumbled.

"What do you mean 'whichever one?'"

"Your gueth ith ath good ath mine," he said, "Well, the mathter theoritht probably hath a muth better gueth than I do."

She smiled at the compliment before the smile faded away. Frowning, William turned his eyes to stare ahead of him.

"She doesn't have to make us *havenesks*, does she?" Frances whispered.

William raised an eyebrow while he shifted his gaze back to her. "What do you mean?"

"I have a theory... and it's probably dead wrong, and I'm probably getting worried over nothing, but hear me out," she pleaded.

"Isabel was explaining that you and Philip were discussing the kidnapped students in the tubes and how Thalassa is making them *havenesks*. But what if she doesn't have to? What if she could make them anything?" she suggested.

"What?"

"What if Thalassa could use her serum to make them and other human beings whatever kind of *alien* she wants?"

William stared up at the ceiling. "I don't know. What would the get out of that?"

"Well, she's bringing *havenesks* back from extinction. So, if any race was in peril of losing abilities, she would have reassurance that she could restore their abilities. We'd be test subjects for an up and coming cure."

"I wouldn't call it a cure."

"She wants to put things how she sees right. We're restored if she can make us *havenesks* or make us serve a greater purpose representing another race."

The gears in William's head slowly turned.

"And if the project is restoration... who's to say that she stops with just altering us? Who's to say she doesn't alter the entire planet to make it what it once was? A clean up project. A habitat appropriate to house the species. What if her plan is to change Earth back to Haven?"

He looked at Frances out of the corner of his eyes. She looked confused and troubled. The possibility that this could be their future was plausible, but it was not a future William wanted to see come to pass.

"How would we prove that?" William asked.

Frances opened her mouth before closing it. "I don't know."

~§~

The two stood outside of the school while waiting for the bus. They were both stuck in their heads and trying to figure out the next course of action. Frances thought it might be good to inform the rest of their group, but William was unsure.

His thoughts were beginning to cloud his mind even more than Thalassa would normally cloud his mind. But Thalassa was always a present force in his head. She never truly left. She could never leave anyone's mind.

"What's become of the *quiznics*?" Frances asked quietly.

"We're gonna lothe Thouth America and then North America will jutht be 'Regular' America," William responded.

"Bill," she urged. He turned to look at her and could see how serious her face was.

"It'th a large death count. It jutht keepth growing. There'th death everywhere- what doeth the think the'th doing? What ith the accomplithing?" he started, growing in frustration and volume.

"It's gonna be okay," Frances whispered as she put her hands to his cheeks and tried to quiet him back down.

"Hey guys!" a voice yelled.

The two turned behind them and as Frances pulled back her hands, William saw that it was Isabel.

"Don't you thtill have your clubth?" he asked.

"I have to pick up Lucas from the preschool and then watch him 'till my grandparents get back," she explained, deciding to stand next to Frances.

"I would've asked you, Bill, but I know that Fridays are usually date nights for the two of you," Isabel said.

"This is going to be a depressing date," Frances reflected as she wrapped her arms around William's waist and put her head to his chest.

"No, it won't," he reassured her. He was reassuring himself too. At this time, he had to be the bigger person. She was stressed and if he was going to be of any help or use, he needed to remain calm.

"What's going on?" Isabel asked.

"The hath a theory about what Thalatha might be doing," William answered.

"Are you guys planning to break in again?" she asked. William could hear the hesitancy in Isabel's voice.

"I don't know what we're planning to do," he said.

"I don't think this is a safe place," a voice quivered.

The three turned behind them.

Eleanor and a few teenagers from Clements were watching Lewis on his skateboard.

"It'll be fine, Eleanor. I'll go for the stairs, do a trick, and land perfectly. Watch," Lewis commanded.

Without even a helmet, Lewis moved towards the staircase on his skateboard. As Lewis passed William, William grabbed Lewis by the back of his shirt and effortlessly picked him up off of the skateboard.

"Dude!" Lewis yelled, as William set him back down on the concrete.

"Dude," William replied, pointing at the skateboard.

As it went down the stairs, the skateboard flipped over and fell on its side.

"Your dad would have killed you if you broke another bone," William reminded Lewis.

A large commotion started, and some students began to point at the skateboard. William turned to look back at it, and Isabel gasped.

Next to the skateboard was a squirrel. It was observing the strange contraption and sniffing around it.

However, as the squirrel turned to look at the crowd, it became obvious that something was wrong. Instead of two black beady eyes, the squirrel had ten. William counted in his head again.

Ten.

"What's wrong?" Frances asked.

"I think you have your proof that Thalatha ith trying to turn Earth back into Haven," William explained.

Chapter 10

Getting out of the truck, William slammed the door. It was the middle of the night, and he looked out at the long strip of road that stretched out endlessly before him. The road was illuminated by the truck's headlights but also the grass' starch white color.

As he looked behind himself, he could see the exact same scene.

He scratched at the back of his head in an attempt to remember where he was going and how he had managed to drive so far out in the middle of nowhere. There were no road markers, and nothing about the place was familiar.

An ominous singing rang in his ears. Scrunching up his face in concentration, William tried to silence the sound but to no avail. He noticed that the road looked a strange purple and blue. More importantly, something about the white grass did not seem to be right.

Slowly, the singing grew louder until William noticed he had unconsciously covered his ears with his hands. He looked around, trying to locate where the singing was coming from.

Stray flowers of all different vibrant colors were singing and swaying in the night wind as they screamed their song.

"Thtop!" William yelled.

The singing only grew louder.

"Thtop it!"

He crumbled to his knees and held his ears as tightly as possible. The noise would not stop. It showed no sign of ever ending. Horrific scream-singing echoed constantly from the flowers. They were out of a pitch and swinging carelessly in the wind.

When William looked up, a stag stood over him. It was large and unsightly with white eyes that peered into his very soul. It loomed over him. The deer tilted its head before rearing on its back legs and stomping down on the road.

"Leave!" it bellowed.

Waking up, William took in a deep breath of air. He was in his room and sitting at his desk. The desk's lamp was on, and it was shining light over his math homework.

Trying to catch his breath, William stared at the text in the book for a while. He blinked a few times and tightly gripped his chest. He was experiencing serious chest pains with his heart pounding against his chest and threatening to break through his rib cage.

As he finally started to feel better, he turned around in his chair to see if Frances had fallen asleep on his bed while trying to do her own studying.

His heart stopped. There was Frances fast asleep; however, sitting on the end of the bed was Thalassa.

Thalassa was in his house.

"How-" he started, feeling his voice leave him.

"William, was it?" she asked. Slowly, she ran a long, bony finger through Frances' hair.

William stood up from his chair, and the back of his hands caught fire. His brows furrowed in anger, although he could feel his fear drying out his throat. Thalassa stared at him, and the two locked eyes as William glared at her.

"You," he growled.

"Me," Thalassa replied.

"What do you want?"

"I want you to stop meddling in affairs that do not concern you."

"I'm right, aren't I?"

Thalassa remained silent.

"You thcared?"

"No, but you should be," Thalassa said before her eyes moved to Frances.

William attempted to take a step forward.

"Uh uh uh. You would not want to hurt the senator's daughter, now would you?" Thalassa whispered, "Such a lovely child. Look at all those beautiful freckles and those chubby cheeks. Is she not just a peach?"

"What do you want?" William asked.

"I thought that would be obvious," she mused.

"What I did- the recordingth- that wath all my fault," he said, "That had nothing to do with her."

"You almost ruined everything," she reminded him.

"Thith hath nothing to do with her!"

"What about those other children with you?"

"What?"

"Isabel Saunders, Roger Crews, Philip Burman," she listed.

"How do you know-"

"How would I not?" Thalassa asked with a sly smile, "You really thought I would not be capable of tracking a few children? Measly, pathetic children who tried to take on my empire?"

William felt the flames on the back of his hands extend as they climbed up his arms. "You thick twithted-"

"Careful. You might burn the house down," she said with a malicious grin.

"Thith wath my fault-"

"It was her plan though, was it not?" Thalassa asked, as she lifted one of Frances' strands of red hair.

"I inithiated it. The didn't want to go through-"

"Well, that is a lie. She just could not, could she? She was stuck with her father in Washington D.C., was she not?"

William was shaking as his brows furrowed further. He had almost completely lost feeling in his legs which had locked long ago.

"You did not need to involve her," Thalassa said.

"Now how would you know any of thith-"

"That is a pointless question. There is a price to pay, Bill," Thalassa hissed, "Surely, you are aware of that."

"I'll pay it-" he started.

"I don't think you can afford to," she whispered as she set her palm aflame.

Slowly, she moved her palm closer and closer to Frances' face.

"Thtop," William whispered desperately.

Thalassa smiled with a wide grin as her eyes flashed orange.

"No!" he yelled.

"Bill," a voice said.

William opened his eyes and quickly pulled his open textbook off of his face. He stared at the night sky as he tried to calm his erratic breathing. Taking in the stars, he noticed that he was laying out in a field.

Frances was mumbling into his chest. He could remember them studying on his bed but not much after. Thalassa did not appear to be anywhere. That much had been a dream.

Wrapping his arms around Frances, William held her close and was comforted by the fact that she was alright. However, he had no idea where they were. His current assumption was that he had teleported them in his sleep.

He imagined his room and the two were back lying in his bed. As he looked around the room to confirm their whereabouts, something else caught his attention.

Bear loomed over the two. The cat stared at William with an enormous smile as it cocked its head from one side to another.

"What are you doing?" it asked.

William found himself unsure how to respond.

"Nice dreams?" the Maine Coon said as its smile only grew larger.

William held Frances tighter. He felt exhausted and slowly he drifted off to sleep again.

Chapter 11

William spent the next several days researching until the point of exhaustion and developing severe headaches, two events which were closely followed by passing out in random places around the house, much to Kate's displeasure. Still, he continued to study up on Thalassa.

For days, William searched endlessly for answers. Schoolwork was a thing of the past as research was now a full-time job.

It was almost midnight, and he was searching through another book to find any new information on Thalassa. As horrible as a place it was, Thalassa's mind was the only place William wanted to be. He wanted to be able to think like her. If he could strategize like the enemy, he could get an advantage.

Apparently, there was a point in time that Thalassa went missing for a while. It was about a year before Caracy died when everything seemed to still be at peace. Common rumors at the time were that she had become pregnant and did not want anyone finding out about an illegal guardian child.

This had to be Llacheu.

The child was never seen directly with Thalassa but sources at The Center, the guardian's place of living, reported a small infant that Gairbith often played with. It was noted that Adonis, himself, started spending more time in the guardian's garden after the child began to take a liking to it.

However, before the child turned even a year old, it went missing. With the child in question gone and no credible eyewitness accounts, all rumors were considered baseless.

As William read the book, he found himself coming to the conclusion that Thalassa had most likely killed the child. William had calculated the date and figured out that the day Llacheu would have turned eighteen was also the day that Thalassa had made her first appearance in China.

Llacheu would have been at *reckoning* age and knowing that must have filled Thalassa with all kinds of guilt. It was probable that she was erasing her son's birthday and the memory of him altogether and replacing the date with her emergence as Earth's savior.

Continuing to read, William stumbled on a passage about a private space pod sent out from The Center around the same time that Llacheu went missing. Most staff assumed Thalassa sent the child away, especially since Caracy and Thalassa seemed more distant upon the first arrival of the mystery baby.

William's brows furrowed, and he scratched at his splint before he took it off. He curled his fingers in before stretching them out all while continuing his reading.

According to the author, there was reason to believe that the child's father was not Caracy. At the time, it was noted that Caracy had removed his wedding ring and no longer seemed quite as close to his wife.

It was thought that Adonis' taking to the child was because it was in fact Adonis' son.

William's eyes drifted back to an earlier passage. A space pod. He wondered if Thalassa had sent Llacheu to Earth. If Llacheu was on Earth right now.

NOT QUITE BROKEN, NOT QUITE PERFECT

Bear leapt onto the kitchen counter.

William tried to push the cat, though it refused to budge. "Move. Off. Down," William said, not bothering to even look at the animal.

A thought struck him, and he turned to the animal. "Hey! Look at me!"

The cat turned its orange eyes and stared straight into William's soul. It smiled its toothy smile and cocked its head to the side as if it was simply an innocent Maine Coon. But William knew the truth.

"You're thuppothed to be with Frank and her parenth at her houthe. You're not thuppothed to be here," William enunciated, "I know your dirty trickth."

The cat's eyes began to wander, and William felt himself become even more irritable. "Look at me!" The cat turned back to him. "You thee that?"

As William pointed his finger at the shotgun on the mantle, the cat amusedly turned its head to look at it.

"You're gonna make me lothe it. And if I lothe it, I will kill you. Gueth what, buddy? My mother ithn't home! I will do whatever I feel like! I will thoot you- do you hear me!" William yelled, "Look at me! I will-"

The cat's neck snapped in William's direction. Its smile was still present, but its eyes were now silver.

Slowly, William's vision clouded until it was silver as well. His mouth opened, but he did not say a word.

"Why would I be here? Why ever would I be here, William?" the cat whispered.

"I..."

William could feel the cat's fur brush against his hands which were pressed onto the table to support him. He wanted to reach out and grab the cat and throw it out of his house.

"How's the reading going? Learning anything?" the cat whispered.

William frowned, becoming angry.

"You have a part in this," the cat said.

"I'm aware-"

"A bigger part."

William scrunched up his face. The gears began to move in his head, and he felt his stomach slowly sink. He could be sick. He might get sick.

"I-..." he began, "That..."

"He thinks! He thinks!" the cat exclaimed playfully. It sounded delighted. It was a cruel malicious delight.

William was silent as his mouth slowly fell more ajar. He squinted his right eye as he felt his heart rate speed up.

"Interesting, isn't it?" Bear asked.

"No. No, you're wrong..." William argued.

"Am I?"

"Admit it. Pleathe. I don't want to play thith game..." his voice cracked.

William closed his eyes which were serving him no purpose already. He was gripping the counter so tightly he was sure his knuckles were white.

"Accept it," Bear cooed.

"I can't. I..."

"Accept it."

"No-"

"Accept-" the cat started again.

William yelled. He was mad. He was beyond mad.

"Maybe next time," the cat said.

William's vision slowly reverted to normal and as he looked around the kitchen, he realized the cat was gone. However, long after it had disappeared, the cat's manic laughter continued to ring and echo in William's ears.

Chapter 12

William was a little more silent than what was normal for him those next few days. He had his quiet days, but the quiet days he found himself in now were full of anger and emptiness.

The cat.

William had shoved his head inside of his locker and had no intention of ever pulling his head back out. He would just stay there for a while until he either was sent to detention or died. Whichever came first. Either was fine.

"Hey," Roger greeted.

Being greeted by Roger had not been a foreseeable option.

"Hi," William mumbled.

"You alright?" Roger asked.

William did not bother to reply.

"Okay then," Roger said to himself, "Right. Uh..." Awkwardly, Roger put his hand on William's shoulder.

"Don't touth me," William said.

Quickly, Roger pulled back his hand. "Do you need somebody to eat lunch with?"

William furrowed his brows and pulled his head out of his locker. "Lunth ithn't until-"

Something hit him in the face. As abrupt as it was to be hit in the face, William still managed to catch it in his hands. He looked down to see a brownie square wrapped in plastic wrap in the palm of his hands.

Raising an eyebrow, William met Roger's gaze.

"It's not made with pot, if that's what you're thinking," Roger said.

"Why would I-"

"You accused me and Philip of being druggies, remember?"

"I only accuthed Philip," William said under his breath.

"Yeah, but you and I both know that you wrapped me in that scene as well," Roger replied with a casual smile. He leaned against a locker and slid down until he was sitting on the hallway floor.

Holding his brownie tightly, William watched Roger begin to unfold the plastic wrap.

Roger looked up. "C'mon. Sit down," he said.

Slowly, William closed his locker door and locked it back up before sliding down and sitting next to Roger. They were silent as they both chewed on their brownies.

"My mom makes brownies probably once every two weeks, and my stepdad and I always finish them in like two days."

"Are you thtill upthet about the stuff I thaid back in November?" William asked.

Roger blinked before turning to look at William. "I mean, not really, no. I think it's funny looking back on all that, but I don't think you still assume that my best friend's a druggie."

"I don't," William admitted, "Okay, I don't mean to be incredibly rude, but I'm about to be, and I don't care. How are you guyth friendth?"

"Does it seem that unlikely?"

"You both are polar oppothiteth."

"I don't know about that. We grew up together," Roger started. "I've known him since I was about four. He told me he was an *alien* and things just spiraled from there, I guess."

"You've known about *alienth* thinthe you were four yearth old?" William asked, as he raised an eyebrow.

"Kinda," Roger replied, "I didn't really believe him for a while. I told my mom, and she explained it was probably his way of coping with his parents' divorce."

William blinked before looking ahead of himself at another locker. "I didn't know hith parenth were divorthed."

"Well, it's not like he flaunts it around or anything. I don't think it was anything serious. From what I know, they just didn't like each other. They were married on *Quod* and when they came to Earth, they decided to leave each other and did so immediately. They hate each other. I don't know why exactly, but the two just can't stand to be in the same room.

"But the divorce definitely took its toll on Philip, and I was perfectly ready to believe that the *alien* stuff was a coping mechanism. I told him to knock it off around middle school, but he actually provided me proof. He showed off a bunch of research books and gadgets his mom had, and it was some pretty good evidence.

"I don't think it blew my mind as much as it should have. It was still mind-boggling, but I wasn't so surprised. But uh to get back to your point," Roger paused, "sure, I guess I've always known."

The boys sat in the hall long after the class bell had already rung. Every now and again, William's eyes would sweep the hall as he looked out for anyone coming by.

"Not that it'th my buthineth, but ith the divorthe the reathon Philip ith quiet?" William asked.

Roger slowly shook his head. "No. He used to be really talkative actually. We used to both be loud and obnoxious, as you would put it."

William frowned.

"But no, Philip's change in personality was more recent. It had nothing to do with the divorce. Or maybe it did, but I wouldn't really know."

Furrowing his brows, William scrunched up his crooked nose. "What happened?"

Roger stopped in the middle of unwrapping another brownie. "It- I-" he started. He tried to turn in William's direction but was met by a penetrating stare.

Sighing, Roger set his brownie down in his lap. "You can't-if I tell you this, you can't tell anyone else. You can't let anyone know I've told you this and especially not Philip."

"Why?"

"Because Philip would kill me, if I ever told a soul."

William nodded.

"Last year was difficult. *Quiznics* are agricultural type *aliens*. They're *plant people*. They like to tend to plants. And last year, Philip's garden died. I don't know why. I don't know what happened," Roger confessed.

He looked shaken up as he told the story. "The plants all died, and it just crushed him. The day they died, he worried about it incessantly at school. It was all he talked about. I walked home with him after school, and we hung out while he tried to fix the garden. He wanted to see if he could grow all the flowers back as fast as possible.

"I should've stopped him. I watched him begin to mess with the flowers, and I was just concerned with doing homework. I was working on my math homework and just trying to figure it out while he was working on his garden. I didn't even pay any attention to him until he was half an hour into the ordeal. And by then, it was too late.

"He was completely silent, and it felt eerie. I looked up, and he was crumbling before my eyes. Literally. *Quiznics* in *reversions* look a little more than dirt. And I watched my best friend turn to dirt and return to the ground before my eyes.

"He was like that for a solid month, I think. It was just dirt but in human form, and it was just trying to keep together. I was terrified out of my mind and finals came, and I flunked everything," Roger said, taking a bite out of his brownie, "I'm repeating senior year right now but you know, it really ain't that bad."

"What wath *reverthion* like for Philip?"

"I'm really not sure," Roger paused, thinking hard, "I can't imagine it was nice. And he didn't come back exactly the same.

"He's quieter now. And he wouldn't use the ability for a while. It scared him too much. The calla lily he made for Isabel back in December was probably the first time he'd grown anything since the *reversion*. Well, beside his garden. He's been growing that back slowly over a long period of time.

"And then, I guess, he also made that daisy when Isabel found out he was an *alien*," Roger added.

William grew stern as he wondered how awful and painful *reversion* had to be.

"The garden has been growing a lot lately, and I think he's proud of that. He's doing better. Slowly. And I'm glad to have him back."

The two were quiet.

"Are you doing better? Not having any plans to stick your head back in the locker?" Roger asked.

William furrowed his brows as he stared in front of himself. "Yeah, I think I'm doing alright."

It was not the truth, but it was not a complete lie either.

"That's good!" Roger yelled, punching William in the shoulder, "See? There's nothing brownies can't fix." Roger stood up and brushed his hands on his green jacket. He offered his hand to William.

For a brief moment, William looked between Roger's hand and Roger's beaming face before William finally decided to take Roger's hand.

As William stood up, the bell began to ring.

"You ready for lunch?" Roger asked with a chipper smile.

William scratched his stubble and mole before nodding. "Yeah, let'th get lunth."

Chapter 13

William trudged slowly through a field. His vision swirled, and it brought him great pain as he held the side of his head with one of his hands. Daisies surrounded him.

He came upon a large hole and stopped. As he craned his head to look into the hole, William raised his eyebrows.

A body was lying in the hole. It was Philip's. It was Philip's body in the hole. Vines were wrapped around his body and slowly pulled him down deeper and deeper.

The hole went further into the ground the longer that William stared at it.

"Philip..." William breathed.

Philip's eyes were closed, and no response came.

"Philip!" William yelled.

Hundreds of faceless creatures swarmed around William's legs. They were small, only a foot tall at most. They had tiny hands with little fists that they beat against William's legs.

"Save him, save him!" they screamed in a hundred, different little voices.

"I can't..." William said futilely, "I... I can't-"

"Useless, useless. Save, save!" they chanted.

"I can't!" he yelled. He shut his eyes tightly and when he opened them, he was somewhere completely new.

William looked around at his surroundings. The air was now completely still. As his eyes darted, he noticed he was in a small room with strange lights hanging from the ceiling.

The lights glowed, growing brighter one second and growing dimmer the next. It was nothing like flickering but a hundred thousand times more peaceful.

The walls were a dark shade of purple, and the carpet was a deep red. William could see an open door to his left but as he tried to move towards it, he realized his legs were stuck. He looked down to see vines wrapped around his feet. They were keeping him stuck where he was.

In front of him was a mirror, but it did not show his reflection. It showed the rest of the room but not him.

The sound of screaming and yelling disturbed the peaceful ambience.

"You cheated on me! Can you not see the severity of that?" a deep voice yelled.

"It was a mistake!" a woman screamed in reply.

"Those kinds of mistakes do not happen! You were perfectly fine with letting me believe that that child was my biological son! Are any of our children actually my biological children?"

"Of course! What are you talking about? Please, take a breath. You are acting hysterical."

"I have every right to be! You have betrayed me, and you have betrayed this entire family!"

William observed the mirror and as he looked down, he saw a child in the mirror's reflection. It was a baby, probably no more than a year old. The child was sitting on the carpet and staring at himself blankly. It was as though he was tuning out the screaming adults with deliberate effort.

"I love you!" the woman yelled.

"Do not lie to me!" the man shouted, "You have never loved me. You wanted me, and you wanted to attain me, and that was all."

"I wanted you to be a part of my legacy!"

"'Of your legacy?' Look around you! Your sons are your legacy! My son and his!"

The child had wild curly, brown hair accompanied by brown eyes. The eyes looked from one place to the next until it appeared that they were looking up at William.

William looked down but outside of the mirror, there was no child.

"I messed up, but that could still be your child!" the woman pleaded.

"He looks nothing like me."

"Maybe he has all of my traits-"

"Even if that was the case, that does not erase the fact that you slept with him!"

"No- honey, please do not take off the ring."

"Do not 'honey' me. You have broken our vows!"

As William watched the mirror, he watched a child run in the room and pick up the baby. The child looked much older than Lucas, maybe ten or eleven. He had dark brown hair and brown eyes which were wide with fear.

"It is going to be okay," the little boy whispered to the baby.

The sound of a door opening reached William's ear, and he turned to the entrance of the door though no one was to be seen. The door that was opened was further out into the house.

"I am here for the child..." another man's voice said.

"What?" the first man yelled.

"I only-"

"You cannot take him away. I do not care!"

There was the sound of heels clicking on the floor, and William turned his gaze back to the mirror. Through the mirror, he could see the back of a woman. She had long brown hair and was wearing a red dress that reached the ground.

"Hand him over," she said quietly to the small boy.

"No- please," the child begged desperately.

"Give him to me!" the woman yelled before ripping the baby from the boy's hands.

"No- mommy! Please!" the boy screamed.

William looked around himself to see that the vines had almost completely restrained him. They had climbed up his torso and were wrapped tightly around his neck. However, they did not stop there. The vines entered his agape mouth and began to move down into his throat.

William tried to yell but no sound would escape his mouth. His eyes were still trained on the young boy in the mirror who had wrapped his arms tightly around himself. The child continued to sob.

"Mommy!"

William woke with a start. He sat up on the couch and looked around. The television was on, and a news show host was shouting.

"Hundreds have been murdered in South America, and thousands in Asia. The *birds* roaming around Mexico are rumored to be flying north. Our United States of America may very well be the next target," the reporter exclaimed.

Taking in a harsh breath through gritted teeth, William gripped his head as it began to pound fiercely.

"What is wrong? Do you not feel well?"

William looked behind himself to see Thalassa standing in the kitchen. He stood up and clenched his fists.

"Why?" he asked.

"Is that all you have to say?"

"I athked a quethtion."

"And I believe I asked one first."

"Why! Why would you do thith? Why any of thith? What do you want from me!" William yelled.

Thalassa stared at him in amusement before a smile creeped up her lips. "Por favor no nos mates."

The words had come from her mouth, but it was not her voice.

"What?" William asked.

"It is your own fault," she said, "Por favor no nos mates."

The first phrase was hers, but the second was not. The second phrase was from another voice, one speaking in Spanish.

William stared at Thalassa with his mouth open, as he tried to figure out how to respond.

"Wake up, William!" Thalassa commanded.

William woke up to find himself standing outside of a mud-hut house in the middle of nowhere. He had never seen this place in his life. No. He had seen it. Somewhere.

It clicked. He had seen it on a news channel talking about the *quiznics* destroying farmland.

Looking in front of himself, William could see a woman who was holding a young girl tightly to her chest. He looked around to see the full moon shining brightly in the open night sky and the destroyed crops around his feet.

He felt his chest sink, as it occurred to him where he was. He had teleported to Venezuela.

"Por favor no nos mates," the woman whispered.

William had learned Spanish from Isabel, and he knew that the woman was pleading for her and her daughter's life. Both the mother and the young girl were shaking violently. They were obviously terrified of him.

William imagined the living room and immediately teleported back.

"How is Venezuela this time of year?" a voice asked.

William turned to see Bear sitting on the coffee table. The cat was smiling a wide, toothy smile, and its tail was swishing back and forth and back and forth mischievously.

"Go away," William said.

The cat faded, though its disembodied smile lingered for a few seconds.

Slowly, William pushed his glasses into his hair and rubbed his eyes as he sat down on the couch. He was so tired.

Chapter 14

William wondered what he was. At first, he was just an *alien* and then he was an *amalgam*. Now, he had no idea what he was. His head was stuck on repeat as it simply played dull words and images over and over again.

Roger had helped quiet the traffic in his mind some. Maybe. William could barely tell anymore. He felt numb.

He sat as still as physically possible in one of the classrooms. Although no one was in the English classroom and no one would be entering it for a long while, he did not want to take the chance of someone seeing him. If he was still enough, maybe he would never be seen again.

He did not want to be looked at by the human eye, and he would keep it that way by any means necessary.

Normally, he would be at chess with Roger and Philip but not today. He knew there was no chance he would manage. He was falling apart at the seams.

Anger grew in his chest to the point that he could feel a burning sensation within him. He pulled off his glasses and rubbed his face furiously. In moments, he felt his face become engulfed in flames. He wanted to fight back, but he was exhausted. He felt no motivation to fight. It felt easier to just succumb to it all and give up.

Thalassa was going to take over and change Earth back into what it once was. She would take over Earth and win. She had won so far. She would win again. There was nothing that could be done.

The sound of the classroom door opening shook him from his thoughts. The fire went out immediately, and William tried to breathe the shallowest breaths possible.

"Bill?" a voice called.

He put his glasses back on before turning to his right and looking up to see Frances. "Frank?"

She reached out for him as she lowered herself to her knees. "We've been looking for you everywhere. Isabel said you didn't show up to chess, and she was worried. What's wrong? What happened?"

"Could you thut the door?" he asked as he pushed his glasses up into his hair and rubbed his eyes in an exhausted manner.

Carefully, Frances pushed the door closed. "Bill, what is going on?"

"Nothing," he lied, putting his face into his hands.

"Bill," she whispered, reaching out and touching his face. She took hold of his hands and pulled them away from his face. "I'm here, okay? You can talk to me. You know that." She moved her hands to his cheeks.

He shook his head defeatedly.

"William," she breathed.

"It'th too muth, Frantheth," he murmured, hollowly, "I have thethe nightmareth, and the cat- Bear ith everywhere jutht haunting me."

Frances slowly wrapped her arms around his neck and held him tightly. "It's gonna be okay," she whispered, "I promise you."

He held tight to her. He only wanted to live in this one moment for as long as he could. He was safe in this one moment.

"I'm not gonna leave. I'm not going anywhere," she consoled, "I'm not gonna leave you."

Slowly, William pulled back. He stared at her lap while trying to collect his thoughts. "Your cat ith doing thomething. I don't know how. I don't know why. But it'th alwayth there jutht plaguing me thomehow."

"Bear?" Frances asked in confusion.

At the sound of its name, the cat meowed.

William stood up, while Frances turned her head around in the noise's direction. The Maine Coon sat on top of one of the tables. It was just leering at the two.

"Kitty?" Frances called out.

The cat jumped from the table and climbed into Frances' lap. Wanting nothing more than attention, Bear rubbed his face into hers.

Frances froze, breathing slowly before she set a hand into the cat's fur. "He…?"

"I don't know," William explained, leaning against the wall. He sat back down while running a desperate hand through his curls. "I don't know."

Picking up her cat, Frances set it down beside her and away from her lap. "How long has he been doing this?"

"Too long- I can't be thure. Maybe *reckoning*?"

She was quiet. She found his arms and ran her hands up them until she located his hands in his hair. As she unlaced his fingers from the knotted curls, she pulled his hands into his lap and held tightly to them.

William stared down at his lap, and his brows furrowed in anger at himself. "I'm a monthter."

"No- hey!" Frances yelled.

He looked up at her and blinked a few times. He had not expected her to yell.

"We don't use that term," she said as her face flushed red, "We don't call ourselves monsters."

"I'm an acthual monthter, Frank-"

"Being *alien* does not-"

"No, you don't get it!" he yelled.

She fell quiet, and William blinked, immediately checking his temper. "I'm thorry. I didn't mean to yell at you. I'm thorry."

"What don't I get?" she asked.

He opened his mouth to try and explain before he let out a long breath. "I'm Thalatha'th thon," he whispered.

Her blank eyes widened. "What?" she asked.

"Thalatha had a thon with Adonith. They thent him away, pothibly to Earth. I think it'th me," he explained, "Thalatha frothe when the thaw me. Adonis frothe, and Ophelia frothe. Ophelia talked with Thalatha about how I looked like Adonith. I-..."

The two were quiet.

"I'm thorry," he whispered.

"You don't have anything to be sorry about," she replied.

"I wath amathed that you could bear me when you found out I wath an *alien*, but thith-"

"This is no different," she interrupted.

"I could be related to a murderouth tyrant."

"You're related to a civil engineer who has raised you on her own since you were ten months old," Frances said, speaking clearly with determination, "You're a child of the Mason clan, a badge you've worn with pride since the day you received it."

His ever-darting eyes looked for anything else to focus on.

"Look at me," Frances whispered.

"I might be-"

"I know you're not. I don't need eyes to know that, Bill."

William shifted his eyes to meet hers. The small brown eyes with their white dots peered straight into his soul. His breath hitched as it seemed like she might actually be staring into his eyes.

"Meow," Bear called.

"Oh hush!" Frances scolded. She scooted closer to William before taking his hands in hers. "I love you. And if you are Thalassa's son, that changes nothing. You're not loyal to her, and I know you would never be. You've proved again and again that you care for me and for your mother and for everyone else on this planet."

She took his right hand and brought it close to her lips before pressing a kiss to his thumb. "I love you, Bill."

Cautiously, William wrapped his arms around her lower back and pressed his forehead against hers.

He wanted to stay there forever. It was a moment of calm within the storm, a storm that was never-ending.

Chapter 15

William sat on the couch with Frances' head in his lap. She had fallen asleep a long while ago, and William wanted to let her sleep for as long as possible. While he flipped through the television channels, he also ran a hand through Frances' auburn hair.

He flipped to a channel and paused. His brows furrowed as he watched the television screen.

"Twenty minutes ago, *archiecs* were sighted in New York City, New York. They immediately started a rampage and set fire to everything in their path. They are now twenty minutes into this rampage and show no signs of relenting their terror," the newscaster said.

Carefully, William moved Frances' head and set it down on the couch as he got to his feet.

"Police have been called, but their efforts are proving futile as the *archiecs* continue in their destruction. While fires grow, firemen are finding it harder to put the flames out."

A video played while the reporter continued to talk. People were running and yelling, but the muted video would not let any of their screams be heard. *Archiecs* were attacking left and right. They were purposefully violent.

As Philip's voice echoed in William's ear, William became angrier.

'In reversion, priority number one is survival.'

This was not survival. This was killing with the intent to kill. This was malice.

After a minute, William realized he had completely tuned out the newscaster. She was discussing Thalassa's reaction to the news, and the video cut to Thalassa back on a podium. She appeared to be in Venezuela. He assumed she had been talking about the *quiznics* but had been informed of the sudden and surprising attack from the *archiecs*.

Sudden and surprising. Right.

The crowd was screaming and yelling. There was no reporter or journalist that was not trying to get Thalassa's attention in the hopes she would call on them.

Thalassa held up her hands in an attempt to quiet the crowd.

"I do not have much knowledge of what is taking place in New York. Please understand this is the first I am hearing of it," a voice translated for her.

William felt anger begin to grow in his chest as he watched. This was not the first she was hearing of it. She was behind the act of terrorism.

"There is so much tragedy!" Thalassa yelled, "I am trying to help, but I can only do so much. I have an army, but I have nowhere near enough resources to help you all. If we were better prepared, we would not be so helpless right now. If my treaty had gone through, I could be providing more aid right now. I only ever meant to help."

She looked sorrowful, but her eyes were as dead as always. She did not feel a thing.

"So many people have stood against me when I have done absolutely nothing wrong. I mean good! But others are out to hurt you. The false video that was created to make me look like a villain has brought nothing but hurt and pain. It has stopped my treaty and stopped your protection.

"Whoever made that video and brought fear and doubt into your minds is a hateful human being. They have hurt you, they have hurt your countries, and they have hurt your planet."

Thalassa looked up into a camera. It was like she was staring through the television and straight into William's soul. William raised an eyebrow. He was doubtful she could see him, but he could not be entirely certain.

"Whoever you are, come forward. Admit that your video was a lie. Can you not see how much pain and suffering you have brought about? I will do everything in my power to help the inhabitants of Earth and restore them to their rightful place, and you will be punished for your crimes," Thalassa said.

William's other brow rose before both eyebrows knitted together in fury. He stared at the television with both anger and determination. He was mad. If Thalassa thought he would readily die, she was wrong. She could blame him as much as she wanted. She could turn the world against him but that would never break his resolve to stop her.

If Thalassa had intentions to kill him, William had intentions to kill her. Someone was going to die, and William would be sure it was not him.

Chapter 16

A repeated knocking came at the door. William opened his bleary eyes and carefully moved off the couch. He approached the door and slowly opened it.

"I need your help-" Isabel started. Her worried expression turned to confusion. "Did you just wake up?"

William furrowed his brows and looked down at his white T-shirt and blue sweatpants.

"Yeah- what do you need my help with?" he asked.

"It's noon. Why are you still asleep?" Isabel asked.

"It'th a Thaturday, and I will live how I want to. If I could have my way, I'd thtay athleep until four or five in the afternoon."

"That's no way to spend a Saturday," she chided.

"What do you want, Morgan?"

"Were you sleeping on the couch?"

"What. Do. You. Want?" William enunciated.

"Roger just called me. Philip isn't doing well," she explained.

William frowned. "What do you mean?"

"I don't know if you're aware, but the *archiecs* attacked New York last night," Isabel explained.

He traced figure eights on the back of his neck. He had no idea why he was tracing when there were no screws, but he still traced. "I'm aware," he said while nodding.

"Bill, the *alien* hospital that Philip's mother works at- it was attacked," she whispered.

"What?" William asked, as his brows rose.

"Roger doesn't know if Philip's mom made it, but he thinks Philip is falling apart out of worry."

"Why do you need my help?"

"You're the only other *alien* we have. And you're a friend."

William's darting eyes looked for something else to focus on. "Yeah. Okay."

Isabel nodded anxiously. "I want to get there as fast as possible, so if you could get ready and we could take the truck-"

Suddenly, William felt something bump into him from behind as a pair of arms wrapped around his waist.

"Who's at the door?" a half-awake Frances asked.

Isabel looked from Frances to William, then back to Frances and finally back to William again. "Did you-"

"No! We jutht camped out on the couth, and we fell athleep at thome point. That'th it," William explained.

"Uh huh," replied Isabel. She looked not only unconvinced but also massively disapproving.

"That'th it- give uth a few minuteth to get ready, and then we'll drive over."

"Okay," Isabel said, as she began to appear nervous again.

~§~

Pulling into Philip's driveway, William killed the engine and got out of the car. Isabel climbed out, and William moved to the passenger side door to help Frances out.

Immediately, Isabel walked around to the back of the house, and William and Frances followed her close behind. At

103

the back of the house, the three found Philip and Roger sitting in the grass and staring at a wilted bed of flowers.

"It's okay, buddy," Roger said. He turned around and noticed the other before trying to give them the best smile he could manage. "Look who's here."

Philip turned to the others. William had rarely seen Philip with anything other than a blank expression. Now, however, William saw Philip almost completely broken. He looked like a shell of himself, like a frightened child.

"Baby..." Isabel whispered.

William frowned at the pet name.

Isabel slowly lowered herself to the ground before wrapping her arms tightly around Philip's neck. "It's gonna be okay."

Returning the hug, Philip buried his face into her neck.

"What happened to the flowerth?" William asked.

Philip pulled his face away from Isabel and looked up at William and Frances. "It..." he started.

"Let's go inside," Roger said, as he stood up.

William raised a brow at Roger before following Roger's lead and bringing Frances along.

"What's going on?" Frances asked.

"Philip has been trying to make contact with his mom and hasn't managed to get a hold of her," Roger started, as he nervously crossed his arms in front of his chest.

"Did she die?" Frances asked.

"Maybe? It's not been confirmed yet."

"Do you think the died?" William pressed.

Roger slowly shook his head. "No, but that's just the optimist in me. I wouldn't know for certain. It's up in the air, and it kinda makes the air hard to breathe, especially for Philip."

"He killed hith flowerth?" William asked, as he turned to look back outside.

"No! No, no, no," Roger said, his face displaying horror, "Absolutely not."

"Then why-" William began, turning back to Roger.

"I don't know why they're dead, but Philip values the sanctity of life. He wouldn't kill the flowers out of anger, or because he can't reach his mother and he's scared she's dead," Roger explained.

"It's a mood garden," a voice piped up.

The three turned to see Philip and Isabel standing in the doorway. Isabel was holding tightly to Philip's arm, and Philip seemed to only be able to stare at the ground.

"A mood garden?" Frances asked.

"The flowers are directly influenced by how I feel. Usually, I'm complacent or maybe mildly happy, and the flowers do fine. But... when I'm depressed... and scared... the flowers wilt..." Philip mumbled.

The five spent the day at Philip's house and the three humans and *amalgam* looked after the *quiznic*. The television stayed on and played cartoons for hours on end. When the silence became too uneasy, the cartoons were at least there to provide some background noise.

William stood leaning against the kitchen counter as he watched over the rest of the room. Roger grabbed a snack from one of the cabinets and began to eat before elbowing William.

Confused, William glared at Roger while Roger made obscure eye glances in an attempt to convey a silent message. With a sigh, William turned his attention to Philip.

"How are you doing?" William asked awkwardly.

Philip looked up across the room at William. "Better," Philip mumbled.

Immediately, a wave of relief seemed to wash over Isabel's face. She smiled softly at Philip.

"That'th good," William said.

Silence filled the room once more.

"Ith it normal for you for the flowerth to die?"

Roger choked on his snack, and Isabel shot William the most furious glare he had ever seen from her in his life. Even Frances rose a brow at his actions.

Philip opened his mouth before shutting it. "I guess. This is the second time it's died within a year."

"What happened the firtht time?" William asked, as Roger turned his eyes to the ground.

"I don't know," Philip admitted, "I was just sad. I was fine and then suddenly, I wasn't, and everything hit at once. Last year should have been my last semester of high school, and it wasn't, because I just fell apart."

"What wath it?"

Philip stared blankly before shrugging. "It just occurred to me one night that nothing was going how I wanted it to. Everything just hit me at once, and I was unhappy.

"So, the garden wilted because it's a reflection of my mood. And I didn't want my dad seeing it, because if he did he would get worried, and he would tell my mother, and that was one less thing I needed. I didn't want them to be more disappointed in me than I already felt they were."

The only eyes on Philip were William's. Roger was still staring at the floor, Isabel was looking down at her lap, and Frances' head was turned up to the ceiling. Everyone was uncomfortable.

"I tried to fix it and cover up the fact I was down," Philip continued although he looked like he wanted to stop, "and I pushed myself too far trying to grow new flowers, and I *reverted*."

William stared at him.

Philip looked up at William before looking away just as quickly. "It was really painful," Philip whispered, "and I'm not sure I came out the same or if I'll ever be the same as I was then."

"You get it. You've experienced that," Philip said.

"*Reverthion?*" William asked.

"No," Philip said, shaking his head in horror, "I mean, you've experienced a change in personality."

"What?" William questioned, as he became more confused.

"Isabel talked about how you changed after your hand broke," he explained.

William looked down at the splint on his left hand before raising an eyebrow and looking to Isabel. "No, I did not."

Frowning, Isabel nodded. "Yes, you did. You're more angry and irritable-"

"I've alwayth been angry and irritable. That ithn't anything new."

"You were heartbroken when you were told your hand broke, and that you couldn't box-"

"I wath upthet, but I wouldn't thay heartbroken-" William argued, as his brows furrowed.

"This isn't a matter to argue over," Frances interrupted.

"No, it ith," William corrected., "becauthe Morgan can't be talking about thingth the doethn't underthtand."

"I'm your best friend of course I understand. Boxing was your life, and you were distraught," Isabel explained.

Roger backed out of the kitchen as Isabel stood up from the couch to argue in William's face.

"Frank, did I thange?" William asked across the room.

Slowly, Frances nodded her head. "Yes."

William frowned before turning back to Isabel.

"You did change," she whispered.

William looked past Isabel to see Philip staring at the splint.

As Philip's eyes met William's, Philip's face flushed red with embarrassment. "I'm sorry-"

"It'th fine," William grumbled, "I'm thorry for lothing it. We're thuppothed to be here for you."

"I'd rather not talk about myself," Philip confessed. His eyes traveled back to the splint. "What happened?"

"I broke it in bocthing. That wath it."

William's attention turned to Frances, and he let out a long exhale. "Kate bocthed when the wath younger, and the thought it'd be thomething I'd like.

"The thtarted me off when I wath about eight. It wath one of the few thingth I enjoyed. I bocthed a lot, and I did it at Clementh High Thcool for a long while."

The darting eyes fixed themselves on the floor.

"I got punthed in the hand during a math, and it wath bad, but I didn't think it wath anything too theriouth. But ath time went by and ath I continued training and bocthing and jutht uthing the hand for everyday thingth becauthe I'm left-hand dominant, it jutht hurt more and more.

"About a year after it firtht thtarted hurting, Kate made an appointment for me, and I got the hand thecked out, and we found out I had broken thome boneth in the hand. The healing protheth wath bad becauthe I had been putting thtreth on the hand for a year, and I now have arthiritith in my hand."

"I'm sorry," Philip said.

"Don't be. You didn't do anything." William frowned, deep in thought. "You're gonna be fine."

Philip nodded. "Yeah."

"You have a lot of friendth who care about you."

Philip smiled weakly as he looked around the room. "I know. I'm really glad to have them."

"Tho am I."

The bell rang, and William's homeroom filled with the sound of discourse as everyone began to talk and move about.

"Alright, alright. Get outta here!" Mr. Delt yelled.

William grabbed his backpack and swung it over his shoulder. With great discomfort, he shoved past several students with Isabel following close behind him.

"Mason!" Mr. Delt hollered before William could leave the classroom.

William turned around before raising an eyebrow. "Thir?" he asked.

He was sure he had not done anything wrong. No, he had done a lot wrong, but nothing that Mr. Delt should have known about.

"I want you to come and see me after you're done with your classes today," Mr. Delt explained in brief.

Frowning, William nodded and left.

"What on earth did you do?" Isabel yelled, as the two walked down the hallway.

"Nothing," William said.

"It can't be nothing."

"I bought fireworkth," William reflected.

"From Randy? Again?"

She was practically screaming in his ear, and it was beginning to get on William's nerves.

"I do. Every week," he continued.

"Why?"

"To blow thtuff up. Ith that not obviouth?" William asked.

"You're gonna get suspended," Isabel murmured to herself.

William shook his head. It was too much of a bother to continue talking.

"You are!" she stressed, "and Randy too if they find out that he's the one selling to students. Or you both might get expelled. How are you going to get into college then, Bill?"

She grabbed hold of both of his arms and tried to shake him. It was a futile attempt, as William was so much bigger than her.

"Calm down!" William finally yelled, "It'll be fine."

He was unconcerned. He was curious, however. He had no idea why Mr. Delt of all people wanted to talk with him.

There were plenty of teachers who would love to give him an earful. The list of teachers who hated him was long. William was no star-student, and he certainly was not any teachers' pet. Yet Mr. Delt put up with him.

Mr. Delt put up with everyone.

For his entire teaching career. Mr. Delt had made an effort to give all students the benefit of the doubt no matter the circumstance. He did not believe in detention, and he made a strong effort to ensure that every student understood his door was always open.

Because of Delt's personality, it was completely out of character for him to ask to see William later.

"He doesn't do this," Isabel argued.

As much as William would rather not admit it, Isabel was right. At the very least, he would not admit it to her out loud.

Hours later, William walked into Delt's office. William cleared his throat in an attempt to get his teacher's attention.

Mr. Delt was looking over some papers but took a moment to motion to a chair. "Take a seat. I'm about done."

William took the seat before resting his head back and staring up at the ceiling. He began to mess with his fingers purely out of sheer boredom but took a moment every now and again to scratch at his beard. The pittering and pattering of the rain outside filled his ears, and he stored the sound in his brain where it bounced around in the empty spaces of his head.

Out of the corner of his eye, William watched his homeroom teacher.

Mr. Delt ran a hand through his brown hair, as he continued to scan his papers. His brown eyes moved rapidly behind his glasses. Shaking his head, the teacher sighed.

"Alright," Delt said as he looked up from his papers, "How are you doing?"

William shrugged. "Alright, I gueth."

"That's good."

"You wanted to thee me?"

"Yeah," Mr. Delt affirmed, "I wanted to know how things are going at home and how you're getting along."

William raised an eyebrow in surprise. "Thingth are okay."

"Are you sure?"

"Why do you want to know?"

Mr. Delt put his hands together and looked down at his lap before meeting William's gaze. "I like to check up on students when they don't seem well, and you've seemed more under the weather."

NOT QUITE BROKEN, NOT QUITE PERFECT

William raised his other eyebrow. He had not been aware that he had been wearing his emotions on his face for everyone to see. Frowning, William's darting eyes moved to the left and looked out of the window.

"You've always been a straight B student in my class, and I know you can do better," Mr. Delt explained.

William knew he could do better too. The thing was that he really did not care. He could not stress how much he did not care.

Uneventfully, William watched a bird hop along a tree branch out in the rain. It was a large black bird. A crow.

"Your mom is a civil engineer if I remember right, isn't she?"

"The ithn't my mom," William muttered without thinking. As he processed what he had said, William straightened up in his seat and turned to Mr. Delt. "I didn't mean to thay that. I thouldn't have."

Delt shrugged carefully, keeping his attention on his student. "It's alright. We all say things that we don't mean to. Have things been tense between you and your mom?"

"Are you a counthelor?"

"No, but I'm sure I'm better than the ones this school has to offer," Delt reflected.

William nodded. It was true. He had a point.

"Your mother went to college and got a degree, but you haven't expressed much ambition for a college career."

Of course, William had not expressed any of his ambitions. William had his own ambitions and intentions, but he did not see how they were necessarily relevant to share with anyone. He liked to keep his business his and his alone.

The crow continued to hop around. It opened its mouth. That was not accurate. That was an understatement. It unhinged its jaw to show off rows and rows of teeth that extended back into its mouth as far as the eye could see.

A *kreshling*.

William raised his brows in alarm. The *kreshlings* had made it out of Mexico and into the States. This was bad.

"Mason, I want to help. I don't want you viewing high school as a burden."

The *kreshling* made eye contact with William. In a matter of seconds, William's vision began to go haywire. He felt his stomach drop as every color began to change, and the world around him gave off a feeling of collapse.

"Bill," Delt started, "I want to help, and I don't know if anything I'm saying is getting through to you, but-"

"Delt," William interrupted, as he closed his eyes tightly, "I apprethiate what you're doing, but I don't think I can be helped. It'th nothing againtht you..."

His vision finally calmed down, and he could see normally again. He turned to Delt and pointed outside. "Do you thee that?"

Delt stood up and looked out the window. "What?"

The *crow* flapped its wings and flew away into the rain.

"Bird," Delt commented.

"Bird," William repeated.

"Are you alright?" Mr. Delt asked with a grimace.

Nodding his head, William rubbed his face and pushed his glasses into his knotted curly hair. "I'll bring the grade up."

"That's not what I asked."

"Can I go?"

Mr. Delt sighed before rubbing his temples. "Yeah. You can go."

Standing up, William picked up his backpack and began to leave.

"Hey!" Mr. Delt called after him.

William turned around.

"You're still my favorite student."

William smirked. "You're thtill my favorite teather."

With furrowed brows, William walked the halls. It took him some searching, but he managed to find Frances standing near the school's front doors and simply listening to the rain.

"Me," he murmured.

"Hey," she said, "I heard Delt wanted to meet with you. What happened?"

"Nothing bad but uh..."

"What?"

William rubbed the front of his neck. "I think I may have theen a *krethling*."

Chapter 18

"Is that it?" Isabel asked, pointing at a bird.

William groaned internally, as he tried desperately to not succumb to his want to roll his eyes.

"No," Philip mumbled, "You're sure you saw one?"

Exaggeratedly, William threw his head forward and backward in a nodding fashion.

The group of five sat outside on the bleachers while watching physical education take place.

"You see anything, Frances?" Roger asked.

As his brows furrowed, William prepared himself to slug Roger in the jaw.

"Not yet. I'll tell you when I do," Frances replied casually.

"Mason, Crews, Burman, Saunders!" Ms. Hill, the physical education teacher screamed, "Get off the bleachers and on the field!"

William stood up with Philip climbing to his feet alongside him.

"I'm not feeling too well, Ms. Hill," Isabel yelled down to the field.

Ms. Hill sighed. "You get a pass, because I know you'd normally participate. But Mason, Burman, and Crews, you three still need to get down."

"I'm pretty sure this falls under physical abuse," Roger commented.

"I don't think it works like that," Frances replied.

"You're not feeling well?" Philip asked Isabel.

"Nah. I just wanna hang out with my girl here," Isabel explained as she hugged Frances tightly.

"What are you even doing here?" Roger directed to Frances, "I've literally never seen you at P.E. ever."

"I wanted to be here in the case you guys actually see the *kreshling*," Frances explained, "Plus, I'm here for moral support. Also, I wanted to actually wear the gym clothes my parents bought for this class, and I imagine I look good in it."

William nodded as he stared at her. She did.

The three boys made their way down the bleachers.

"Are you sure you didn't just see a regular crow?" Philip asked.

"No, I freaked everybody out over a regular crow cauthe I thought it'd be funny- what do you think?" William yelled.

Philip flinched uneasily. "Sorry."

"It's like bird watching but more aggressive," Roger observed, "Look, bird!"

It was a red cardinal. It was not even the bird they were looking for.

William stood with the two on the field. His eyes scanned the skies as he searched for the *crow*.

"Bird!" Roger exclaimed.

"If you thay 'bird' one more time, I will kill you," William explained.

"Why on earth would *kreshlings* be here? If they crossed the border, they would have been sighted in Texas first. How did one get all the way to Georgia without anyone noticing?" Philip mumbled out loud.

"That's hoping it's just one," Roger replied, "Do they not fly in groups?"

"I'm not sure," Philip answered, "The ones that were seen in Mexico were all together, but that's a lot of *reversions*. Usually, a *reverted kreshling* would just exist on its own."

William shifted his eyes to the top of the bleachers. Isabel was droning on about something, and Frances was smiling. If she could still see, her eyes, which were hidden behind her sunglasses, would be staring up at the clouds.

Perhaps he really was nothing more than insane. Maybe he had not seen the bird at all, and it was a trick of the mind. Maybe Thalassa had given up.

Now that was insane.

"Mason, I know you have a good arm," Ms. Hill yelled.

"Had," he corrected, "Patht tenthe."

Ms. Hill was quiet as she glared him down. "Just throw the football, Mason." She tossed a football at him which William easily caught.

"Throw the football, Mason," Roger whispered in a mocking tone.

William faked out throwing it at Roger which caused Roger to tense. William smiled slyly.

"You're a jerk," Roger decided, as he narrowed his eyes at William.

It was nothing William had not heard before, but he kept up the smile.

Later in the day, the five rode the bus home. William fell asleep in his seat and only came back to consciousness when Isabel shook him awake.

"We're in Timbers," she announced.

"Great," William replied, as he got up. He turned to his left and saw Frances.

"What are you doing?" he asked.

"What?" Frances started.

"Is this the stop?" Roger asked.

William turned behind himself to see Roger and Philip. "What are you both doing here? Why didn't you get off at your thtop?"

"I thought we were following you to do more bird watching," Roger explained. Philip nodded in agreement.

"No," William said, "That wath never ethtablithed."

"Well, we're here now," Roger said.

William turned to see Isabel and Frances exiting the bus before following after them. He followed after them and quickly thanked the bus driver as he got off the vehicle. Roger and Philip stayed close behind and filed off the bus along with the rest of the Timbers teens.

"I'm not driving you two back to Clementh," William said to Roger and Philip.

"Oh but you'll drive her?" Roger asked, pointing to Frances.

"Yeah, cauthe the'th my girlfriend," William said.

"Eh," Roger and Philip said in unison.

With a sigh, William took hold of Frances' hand and headed for his house. He intertwined his fingers with hers, and she pressed her chubby cheek into his arm.

When he reached the house, he pulled out his keys before turning around to see the rest of the group again.

"Go home," he instructed, "There'th no point."

"We can still look out for the *kreshling*," Philip said.

"No, we're not gonna do that."

"Are you giving up?" Roger asked.

"I don't thee a point in thearthing for a bird. We've obviouthly lotht, and there'th no point."

"Well, hang a second," Roger started to argue, "I didn't take you for giving up that easily."

"I'm not giving up. I'm jutht tired," he explained, as he swung the door open.

"C'mon! Justice never sleeps!" Roger pointed out.

"We're not juthtithe!" William yelled. He threw up his hands before walking into the house.

"Bill, we believe there's a point in doing this," Isabel said in a calm voice.

"I don't," he replied, as he leaned back against the island counter, "or not right now at leatht. I've barely thlept in dayth. I jutht need a break."

Roger laid down on the couch. "Bird watching is kinda like a break."

"It'th not," William growled, as he glared at Roger.

"You're gonna feel more relieved if we find it as fast as possible," Philip argued.

"I will abtholutely not!"

"Bill," Frances started.

William turned to Frances and stared at her face before his darting eyes moved to her hair, the clip in her hair, her eyes, and back to her full freckled face. As he looked at her, he caught himself glaring and turned away. He was not about to stop glaring, but he did not want to be glaring at her.

"Let's just work together and search for it a little longer-" Isabel started.

"You can thearth all you want- I'm done," William explained. He walked to the back door and slid it open before stepping out into the backyard. He threw his hands up into the air as the rest watched from the porch. "Thearth all you'd like. I'm done. I've had enough."

"You're not the happiest camper," Roger observed.

"Thut it!" William yelled.

"Bill please," Frances called out.

"I'm thick and tired of thith. I jutht-" William started.

Something grabbed at William's legs, and his brows rose in alarm. He looked down to see *vines* climbing up his legs.

Isabel screamed, and Roger began to cuss in terror. The two's reactions threw Frances into a panic.

"Bill!" Philip yelled, as he jumped off the porch.

William yelled out in anger and set his feet on fire. The *vines* tried to escape as fast as possible, but the fire quickly consumed them. After he was sure the *vines* were dead, William quieted the fire.

"Did you do that?" William yelled at Philip.

"No!" Philip squeaked.

With furrowed brows, William grimaced and pulled off one of his sneakers before throwing it at the wall of the house.

"Hey!" Isabel screamed, as the sneaker narrowly missed her.

William pulled off the other scorched and hole filled sneaker and threw it as well. "Thothe are my only thoeth, and now they're burnt..." He cursed under his breath. There was nothing left of his socks.

"There'th a can of gatholine in the laundry room. Thomeone go and get it," William instructed.

"What's going on?" Frances asked.

"*Quiznic vines* tried to grab a hold of Bill," Philip explained.

"What?" Frances yelled.

"Are they clothe by?" William asked Philip.

"*Vines* can stretch for thousands of miles. I have no idea where they might be," Philip explained.

"Will thomeone get the gatholine?" William yelled.

"Why?" Isabel asked.

"Cauthe I'm gonna thet fire to the yard!"

"Are you insane?" she screamed.

"No, I'm not inthane! Thothe thingth jutht grabbed hold of me, and I'm not letting anymore get on my property. Nothing ith about to grow here." His darting eyes glanced over his jeans. The ends had been eaten away by the fire.

"Where's the laundry room?" Roger asked.

"Off the thide of the living room," William said.

Roger nodded before running inside.

William scanned the ground waiting for another attack. Philip scanned with him while mumbling a series of curses beneath his breath.

"I got it!" Roger yelled, holding up the gasoline can.

"Toth it!" William instructed.

Roger threw the can to William, and William immediately set to work. "Everyone back up," William commanded. He walked around the backyard and poured out the gasoline.

"Bill, this is really dangerous," Isabel said, with fear shining through her voice.

"Not for me," William replied.

As he set his foot on fire, he touched the line of gas, and the yard lit up in flames. William reached out his hands and slowly calmed down the flames as he focused as hard as he could.

The flames disappeared and left only dead, scorched grass in their trail.

William breathed heavily before turning to the others.

"Yikes," Roger mumbled.

Wiping his sweaty forehead with the back of his arm, William took in long, deep breaths as he stared at the wreckage. The Maine Coon slinked around the side of the house before sitting and staring up at William with a large, ugly smile.

William frowned.

2 February 1994

Chapter 19

William, Frances, and Roger sat outside of the grocery store as Philip and Isabel picked up ice cream inside. The night before Kate had been less than pleased to see the destruction that had come to her yard; however, after finding out what had happened and that the yard's ruin would keep her and her son safe, she was a little more understanding.

"What are you looking at?" Roger asked.

The darting eyes were not looking at anything. William shrugged.

"He's just staring into space," Frances explained.

"How do you know that?" Roger asked, "It's like you can read his mind."

"Or maybe it's because he lives in his head, and I've been dating him long enough to know that," she replied.

"What's he thinking about right now?"

Frances turned her head in William's direction. "Probably nothing. His head's a little empty."

She was not wrong.

So much had occurred in so little time, and William could barely process anything anymore. He was too exhausted to try. He practically felt brain dead.

Frances pressed a kiss to his cheek, and he let himself enjoy the moment. It was a comforting moment in a storm of everything uncomfortable and painful.

He gently pulled her head a little closer to him and pressed a kiss into her hair.

"Mhm," Frances said contentedly.

"You know? I really kinda wish I had what you both have and what Philip and Isabel have," Roger said.

Frances grew silent, and William actually bothered to turn his attention to Roger.

"You'll find a girl," Frances reassured him.

"I hope," Roger mumbled.

"Listen to me," she continued, "If a blind girl can find someone, and somebody like him can find someone, you'll find someone."

"What do you mean 'thomebody like him?'" William asked, knowing she was referring to him.

"I love you," Frances said, as she leaned back into him.

William wrapped his arms around her front and rested his head on top of hers. "Uh huh."

As he continued to observe his surroundings, he noticed a man with a black goatee and curly black hair that reached the end of his ears. The man was a ways away, but he was walking towards the grocery store.

"Philip," Isabel giggled, as she exited the store.

"I didn't say anything wrong," Philip argued with a nervous smile.

"Yes, you did!" she said, still laughing.

"What'd you say?" Roger asked.

"I just-" Philip started.

"We don't care," William interrupted, his eyes still trained ahead of himself.

"You don't have to be like that," Isabel chided, disapprovingly.

"We really care about whatever it was," Frances spoke up.

"It's not that. I just don't understand why he has to be so rude. Some of us are trying to keep lighthearted right now, and I don't think there's anything wrong with that," Isabel explained.

William was not paying attention. His brows furrowed while he watched the approaching man. Searching his head, he tried to remember why the man looked so familiar.

As much as he wanted to brush it off, he could not. He was certain he had seen hundreds of men throughout his life wearing things as simple as hoodies and baggy pants and looking terribly disheveled.

Disheveled.

William's mind began to clear and as he pictured the man with a pair of large wings and wearing a black tabard, it clicked.

Nagelfar.

Isabel sighed. "Well, we got the ice cream so-"

"We need to go," William said.

"What?" Frances asked.

"Where are we going?" Roger inquired.

For the life of him, William had no idea why Nagelfar would be in Georgia or out in the open. Maybe his eyes were playing tricks on him, but he was doubtful of such.

"Nagelfar," he said.

Philip looked around before seeing the man. His eyes widened. "That's Nagelfar."

"Who?" Isabel asked.

"What? You mean the guardian?" Roger asked in alarm.

"Get inthide," William ordered.

Frances stood, giving William the chance to get to his feet before he pushed her inside of the grocery store. He did not want to be so rough with her, but they were in a hurry.

"Are you absolutely sure?" Isabel asked, as the five filed into the store.

"It's unmistakable," Philip breathed. His voice was full of panic.

There were already not many people in the store, but William still ventured further into the back.

"What are we going to do?" Isabel asked.

Taking Frances' hand, William looked behind himself, as Nagelfar entered the store.

"Take my hand," William growled.

"Who?" Roger asked.

"Everyone."

He turned a corner where they were invisible from human eyes as well as cameras. Thinking of his house, William focused on getting everyone out alive.

Nagelfar rounded the corner and was upon them, but he was too late.

The five were standing inside the Mason house.

"Are we okay?" Isabel screamed.

"What happened?" Frances asked.

"We're safe," Philip consoled, "Bill teleported us to his house."

"Are you okay?" Frances asked William.

"I'm fine," William said. He felt a little tired and uncomfortable, but he was not throwing up blood or dying so that had to be a good sign.

"Bird," Roger said.

The four turned to see where he was pointing. On the other side of the living room window sat a *bird*. Its jaw was unhinged, and it showed the teenagers its several sets of teeth.

William furrowed his brows in anger before making his way to the living room mantle and grabbing Kate's shotgun. He grabbed a shotgun shell and loaded the weapon.

"What are you doing?" Roger asked.

"Wh- Bill!" Isabel yelled.

William approached the front door before swinging it open. He walked outside, and the *crow* turned and stared at him, as William took aim and fired.

The *bird* fell, dead.

"That'th a warning for the retht!" William yelled to the group, "And if Nagelfar thowth hith ugly fathe again, I'll give him the thame fate!"

Looking back at the *bird's* corpse, William watched Bear step over the *bird* gracefully before the cat displayed a wide and toothy smile.

"I'll thoot you too," William threatened.

3 February 1994

Chapter 20

On Thursday, Philip's mother finally reached out to Philip and assured him that she was alive and well. Although Philip would normally look after Lucas on Thursdays at 'Little Adventurers,' Isabel thought it would be better for him to go and see his mother.

In his place, both William and Roger looked after Lucas as helpers at 'Little Adventurers.' William felt he could keep Lucas safe and was determined to look after him. However, if William could have had it his way, he would have kept Lucas at home.

Kreshlings were on the loose, and it worried William that more *birds* were in Georgia and that they were looking to snatch up more children.

"This way!" Lucas yelled, as he tried to drag William away from the group.

"No- Luc," William tried to argue.

"Philip lets me," Lucas protested.

"Well, Philip ithn't here," William explained.

Lucas began to pout as he folded his arms across his chest.

"He makes a compelling point," Roger said.

"No, he doeth not. The anthwer ith thtill no," William said.

He was tired. He was so tired. Dealing with an angry and stubborn five-year-old was not something William needed at that moment.

"Please? Please, please, please?" Lucas whispered.

"That's a whole lotta pleases," Roger observed.

Sighing, William turned his weary eyes to the sky. He blinked in surprise and immediately woke up.

Thousands of feet in the air was an *alien* ship. William was sure of it. It was Thalassa's mothership in the air.

Lucas continued whining, but William had tuned him out. He was trying to figure out what to do. He could teleport into the mothership but certainly not in front of Lucas.

As he considered what to do, something appeared in the sky, and William pushed his glasses closer to his face, while his eyebrows furrowed in concentration.

The speck grew larger but it appeared to still be rather far off. It looked like a person.

A person. William knew he could not be making an assumption like that, but there he was making that very assumption.

The person fell behind a cluster of trees and disappeared as the woods laid claim to them.

"Roger, take Lucath back to the group," William said.

"What?" Roger asked.

"Bill!" Lucas whined.

"Now," William growled through gritted teeth.

"Okay," Roger said hesitantly. He took Lucas' hand and started to pull the preschooler back to the group.

William went into the forest. He walked deeper and deeper as he tried to find what he was looking for. After a few minutes of walking deep into the woods, he stopped and looked around himself.

"Bill!" a voice yelled.

William turned around to see Roger running towards him, and William's eyebrows rose.

"What are you doing? Where ith Lucath?" William asked.

"I left him with one of the other helper's groups. Why'd you run off?" Roger asked.

"I thaw Thalatha'th thip."

Roger's eyes widened. "What?"

"I thaw her thip, and I thaw thomething or thomeone fall from it. Come and help me find them."

The two ventured further in until they finally found what they were looking for.

In the middle of the woods was a bloody girl. William noticed her short black hair and her thin frame and identified her almost immediately as one of the Chinese students.

"Is she dead?" Roger asked. His eyes were filled with horror, and he cautiously approached the girl.

As William looked behind his back, a loud noise caught his attention. He whirled back around to see the girl with her eyes wide open as she desperately gasped for air. She reached out helplessly before grabbing Roger's arm and managing to pull him closer to her.

William was ready to pull Roger away, but the girl's terrified eyes made him pause.

"Thalassa," she whispered. She said something in Mandarin rapidly before her eyes rolled into the back of her head. Her grip around Roger's arm loosened immediately before she fell back and laid limp on the forest floor.

"Is she dead now?" Roger whispered slowly. He lowered himself to his knees and looked her over.

William grimaced as he looked at the girl before he considered what to do. He hated making decisions. If he left her here, she would certainly die. She had already lost a lot of blood, and he could see that she was bleeding from her head.

Gritting his teeth in frustration, William put his hand on her arm and visualized the *alien* hospital in New York. He could see the lobby clearly. There were the chairs and the reception desk along with the transport desk where a *nebulan* was waiting to serve as a personal ambulance.

As William turned to his right, he saw that Roger had been holding onto the girl's other hand and had teleported with William.

"What did you do?" William asked.

"What did you do?" Roger asked.

There was a pit in William's stomach. He felt bad. He felt wrong, but at least he was not puking up blood or dying.

"Can I get thome help?" Willliam called out.

The receptionist stood up and looked over her desk at the two boys and the bleeding girl before punching a few numbers into a phone.

"Assistance needed in the lobby. All available medical personnel, assistance needed in the lobby," the woman said into the phone.

"Mason?" a voice called.

The two boys looked to the left to see Dr. Haming. The blonde woman immediately knelt down and stared at William's face. "Vhat-"

"Not me," he said to the German woman, "Her."

It was as though Dr. Haming had not even noticed the bleeding girl until that moment. It was exactly that. Philip's mother looked to the girl and the color immediately drained from her face.

She began yelling in German and several nurse aids gathered around her. They pushed William and Roger away and began to attend to the girl.

"Do you know her name?" Laura Haming asked.

The two climbed to their feet before shaking their heads.

"How did you find her?" she pressed.

"The fell," William murmured, "Thalatha'th thip."

Laura's eyes widened in horror before she yelled some more in German.

William and Roger watched as the girl was carried away.

"Hey!" a voice yelled.

The two turned to see Philip who was dressed in scrubs. "What's going on? What're you guys doing here?" Philip asked.

"We found a girl," Roger explained.

"A girl?" Philip questioned.

"She might've been thrown out of Thalatha'th thip," William said.

Philip's eyes widened in horror. "This has really just been a horrifying week, hasn't it?" he whispered.

A transport approached William and Roger. "You need help gettin' home, chaps?" the transport asked with a thick British accent.

William started to shake his head before Roger tapped him on the shoulder.

"Is it okay if I stay here?" Roger asked.

"What? Why?" William asked.

"To make sure 'Jane Doe' is okay and stick around with Philip for a bit," Roger explained.

Slowly, William nodded. "That'th fine."

William turned back to the transport. "I'm alright. I can make it back mythelf."

He envisioned the woods and was back in Georgia. As he started to venture back out of the woods, he heard the sound of screaming. William's heart skipped a beat and immediately he broke into a sprint.

"Lucath!" William yelled, as he ran for his life.

Exiting the woods, William looked to the sky to see dozens upon dozens of *crows* flying around in the air. Children were screaming, and the helpers seemed to be trying to protect the children, but William was unsure how much they could do. There was no defending against these monsters.

"Lucath!" William shouted.

"Bill!" a voice screamed.

William looked to see the brown haired, gray eyed little boy running towards him. Immediately, William ran and closed the distance before scooping the boy into his arms and holding him tightly.

"What's happening?" Lucas asked.

Lucas tried to move his head, but William had a firm hold of the back of Lucas' head.

"What's happening?" Lucas yelled.

"Thtop moving, Lucath!" William commanded.

"I want to see!"

"No, you do not!" William yelled.

William had to get Lucas out and fast but there was a high chance that if William teleported, everyone would see him. However, time was of the essence, and William had no other options.

NOT QUITE BROKEN, NOT QUITE PERFECT

A *crow* dove down and picked up one of the small children who screamed helplessly.

As William watched in horror, Lucas pulled his head from William's grip for an instant. William grabbed hold of Lucas' head and turned the child's eyes away, but it was already too late.

With the boy's head firmly pressed into William's shoulder, William visualized Lucas' bedroom, and the horrific scene faded away. Lucas was safe.

William was breathing heavily and trying to remain as calm as possible, but the event he had just witnessed would not stop flashing before his eyes. Lucas was screaming. The preschooler had seen far too much.

"Lucas!" Isabel yelled.

She opened the door and stared at William and her brother. "Lucas?" she whispered much more softly.

Slowly, William handed the crying five-year-old over to his sister. Isabel held her brother tightly and looked between Lucas and William.

William put a hand over his mouth, but his hand slowly slipped away.

"What happened?" Isabel mouthed.

William shook his head. It was the only reply he could offer.

~§~

Later in the evening, William, Frances, and Isabel were gathered in William's living room.

"Ith Lucath okay?" William asked.

"Not really. He was still crying when I handed him over to my grandparents," Isabel explained.

"Doeth he know I teleported?"

"I don't know. He was pretty traumatized- I'm not sure he understands what happened today. I don't understand what happened today."

"I'm tho thorry," William apologized.

"What happened?" she asked.

"I had Roger take him back, and Roger left him in the care of one of the other helperth. We found a girl in the woodth-"

"What?" Isabel asked, shocked.

"Thalatha'th thip wath overhead," William said.

"She threw a girl from her ship?" she whispered.

"Maybe. It looked like one of the college thtudenth from firtht imprethion."

"What happened?" Frances asked.

"I teleported her to the hothpital. Dr. Haming hath her now."

"Where's Roger?" Isabel asked.

"He wanted to thtay with Philip and keep tabtht on the girl to make thure the wath doing okay."

"And then the *kreshlings* attacked?" she assumed.

"I got back and there wath yelling, and it wath a whole nightmare. I thould have thtayed with Lucath, or I thould have made Roger thtay with him. I thould never have left him alone."

Sighing, William sat down on the living room floor. "I'm tho thorry, Morgan."

"It's alright," she mumbled.

It was not. Everyone knew it was not.

Bear climbed into William's lap before sitting there and smiling up at him.

Annoyed, William picked up the cat and set it away from himself. He was not in the mood now or ever.

"I'm gonna go back to the hothpital," he said.

"What? Why?" Frances asked.

"The girl had thome connecthion with Thalatha even if it wath jutht ath a tetht thubject. If thith girl wath being harmed by Thalatha, think of how muth political ground we could gain. If we could prove that Thalatha ith abducting and hurting human beingth againtht their will..."

This girl, whoever she was, needed to help the group. She could very well be the key to upending Thalassa's game. The odds might finally be in Earth's favor.

Chapter 21

"Her name is Nina, but that's all I've gotten out of her," Roger explained, "She hasn't said much since she's gotten here, but she did try and attack me which was great."

"Are you okay?" Isabel asked.

"Oh yeah, I'm fine," Roger reassured her, "There was only a box of tissues available to her which y'know she threw at me. And then I sang kumbaya, and she seemed to relax after that."

William had no idea whether or not Roger was joking or completely serious.

"You guys can come in and talk with her, if you'd like," Philip said, as he poked his head out of the room.

The four entered the hospital room. Nina looked in slightly better shape. Her dark, raven-black hair covered some of her face, but she looked at peace.

Roger sat down in a chair next to the bed, one he had probably moved next to the bed earlier.

"Have you athked her anything about Thalatha?" William asked.

"No," Philip admitted, "Mostly, she's been really angry when she's woken up, and we've been trying to get her water and a bit of food. She hasn't said much, but I don't know whether it's because she's just trying to recover right now or if she can't speak English."

Isabel hugged Philip tightly, and he held her close as he stared at Nina.

"This feels a bit wrong. Aren't we exploiting her?" Isabel asked.

Slowly, Nina took in a long breath of air before opening her eyes. Her eyelashes fluttered, and she looked around the room at her unexpected guests.

Everyone's eyes were on her, as it seemed they were all unsure of what to do.

"Can you thpeak Englith?" William spoke up.

Nina's face grew stern.

"I don't know if she understands," Roger confided, "They are not here to harm you. And you already know that Philip and I aren't gonna hurt you."

"How are we to get any information about Thalassa out of her?" Isabel asked.

Nina apparently registered the word Thalassa, as her eyes widened.

"It's okay! It's okay!" Roger reassured her, "We want to stop Thalassa."

"You guys are wanting to stop her?" Nina asked.

She spoke.

"Aren't you?" William questioned.

"Mason?" a voice called.

The five turned to see a blonde woman standing in the doorway.

"Mom?" Philip asked.

Dr. Haming's attention turned to her son before she furrowed her brows. "You know not to be here," she said.

Philip's face flushed red in embarrassment.

"We were just trying to see if we could ask her about what Thalassa was doing," Roger said, as he gestured to Nina.

"No. No! Out!" Dr. Haming yelled.

Nina watched as her guests began to leave, but she grabbed Roger's arm just as he got the chance to stand.

"I want to talk to him," Nina said.

"You vant him to shtay?" Dr. Haming asked. She looked to be in disbelief.

Nina nodded assertively.

Roger's eyes widened in surprise as he looked from one member of the group to another.

William tilted his head as if to tell Roger that he might as well stay. If Nina wanted him, there was no point in arguing. Plus, they might manage to find something out. It was better for one of them to talk with her than all five to be stuck on the outside.

Hesitantly, Roger nodded and sat back down in his seat.

"Ze resht of you. Out," Dr. Haming said through gritted teeth.

The four filed out as Dr. Haming closed the door behind them. They stood in the hallway with William holding tightly to Frances and Isabel holding tightly to a somewhat terrified Philip.

"All of you go to ze front," Laura ordered.

The four started to leave.

"Mason!" Laura yelled.

William paused and turned around.

"You come here," she ordered.

William slowly released his hold of Frances while Philip and Isabel continued to sheepishly make their way to the waiting room. Although he had let go of Frances, Frances still held onto William's sleeve and followed after him.

"Vhy are ze *nikolates* gone?" she asked, as she gestured to the back of her neck.

William furrowed his brows as he scratched at his beard. "I don't know," he admitted, "They've been gone for a few weekth."

"You turned zem off?" she asked, as she examined the back of his neck.

"No, but thomeone did," William replied.

"Vell," she started, "zis is… good. You can shtart *nikolates* as the tranink tools zey are."

William nodded. "When would you want me to thtart?"

"Sometime in the followink veek. You brink your mozer vis you, and ve can discuss it."

With that, she left the two alone.

"It's gonna all be okay," Frances whispered happily.

"We gotta make it through thith Thalatha fiathco firtht," William muttered.

"You guys gotta get in here," Roger said, as he poked his head out of the room.

"Hey!" William yelled down the hall.

Philip and Isabel turned in his direction. William motioned for them to follow before leading Frances in the room.

Nina was sitting straight up in the bed. She looked fierce and determined, as she looked around at the five. "Thank you all for bringing me here, but I need to be dismissed from this hospital as soon as possible."

"The hospital can get your parents," Philip offered.

"I'm not interested in that," Nina explained, "I have to get back to Thalassa's ship."

William raised a brow. "You want to go back?" he asked.

"I have to. I need to get back on that ship."

"Do you have any idea what the wath doing to you on that thip?"

"Do you?" she shot back.

"Yeah!"

"It's on video," Isabel spoke up.

Nina looked perturbed. "Thalassa was videotaping us?" She appeared disgusted and fearful.

"No, that'd be awful," Frances said, "We snuck onto the ship and tried to show the world what atrocities Thalassa was committing."

"I did," William mumbled to her.

"Yeah, I know," Frances whispered.

"Wait. You've successfully snuck on before?" Nina questioned.

"Conthidering we're all alive, yeah," William replied.

"We could show her the video," Roger suggested, "Do you still have it? Or would Ella?"

"I think Dave has it, doesn't he?" Isabel asked.

"Abtholutely not. Ella took it, but I altho made thure that it'd be thmoething Dave never thaw on hith video camera. If he thaw that on hith camera, he would realithe I got into the thip and thuthpect me of being an *alien*," William explained.

"You're an *alien*?" Nina asked.

The five looked to her.

"You're in an *alien* hospital," Philip explained.

"What? Why?" she asked.

"Cauthe you fell from Thalatha'th thip," William said bluntly.

"There are *aliens* on Earth who do not stand with Thalassa. We tried to stop her, and we took a video proving the detestable practices she was up to and what she was doing to you and your friends," Philip continued.

"What was she doing?" Nina asked.

Philip looked to William for an answer. "It'th pothible the wath mething with your and your friendth' DNA," William explained.

Nina's eyes widened.

"Would Kate have taped the video on the VHS?" Isabel asked William.

William raised both of his brows at her before slowly nodding. "The might have."

"We could show her the video," Roger said, nodding his head towards Nina.

"I don't know if we could bring your mom's VHS system to the hospital," Frances confided to William.

"We could take her to your house," Roger said to William.

"What?" William asked.

"She can see the video and see what's going on, and then we can take her to the ship."

"No, we're not going to the thip. Why on earth would you want to go there to begin with?" William asked Nina.

"My friend is still on that ship," Nina said, "I have to get her back."

"We're not a rethcue team."

"We could be," Frances offered.

"Thith ithn't about goodwill!" William yelled, "Thith ith about bringing an end to a tyrant!"

"We're gonna help you get your friend back," Isabel said to Nina.

"I still want to see the video if that's alright," Nina said.

"Ith no one lithtening to me?" William asked.

"If we go, we'll have to be prepared," Frances said.

"Wait, hold on a second," Philip spoke up, "She isn't even ready to be released from the hospital yet.

"So, we sneak her out," Isabel said mischievously.

William had never expected Isabel, the girl who followed the rules to the letter, to be a rule breaker at that moment. Yet here she was trying to convince Philip that they should break Nina out of the hospital.

"How are we supposed to do that?" Philip asked with a touch of nervousness in his voice.

Isabel turned to William, and the two locked eyes. William groaned and let out a long sigh. "Fine."

"Wait what?" Frances asked.

"We doing this, big man?" Roger asked with an excited smile.

William glared at Roger before turning to Nina. "How do you feel about teleporting?"

"Teleporting?" Nina asked. She looked at his extended hand and cautiously took it. William could see just how much smaller her hand was in comparison to his. Or maybe his hand was just huge.

"Yeah," Roger yelled before he touched William's shoulder.

Isabel touched William's other shoulder before taking Philip's hand while Roger reached his hand out for Frances. The six had made a chain. William imagined the living room of his house, and all six were transported to the Mason house.

NOT QUITE BROKEN, NOT QUITE PERFECT

"Meow!" Bear screamed.

The six's attention turned to the cat that was watching them from the island counter.

145

Chapter 22

Nina sat on the couch while she watched the entire community. Frowning, she held one of the couch's sad and decrepit pillows tightly to her chest as her eyes swept the room.

Roger and Isabel sat near the television and rifled through a box of tapes. Frances was staying close to the two, and Philip was close to Nina so he could help her by any means he could should any health problems flare up. He was still unhappy that the group had moved her from the hospital.

William stood and watched over his group.

"This one?" Roger asked.

"Yeah," Isabel said, as she took the tape from him.

Frances reached out for her cat as Bear passed her. She began to stroke his fur before lifting him to her face. "Speak!" she yelled.

Since Frances had found out that the Maine Coon was particularly suspicious, she had become ten times as fascinated with it.

Bear looked grumpy as ever as Frances shook him delicately.

The cat turned its attention to William who only smiled slyly. He could only think that the animal was getting what it right so deserved. It made William happy.

Isabel inserted the tape and fiddled with the remote until she finally made the tape play.

The video started with a group of kids William did not know. However, after a few moments, the camera turned and focused on a couple dancing together.

"Oh, this isn't the right tape," Isabel observed.

"It'th gonna be the motht rethent," William said, as he furrowed his brows in confusion. He had no idea what he was watching.

"None of these are marked accurately. This one was marked 'William video,'" Isabel explained.

"Kate recordth over thingth all the time and doethn't thange the label. You're looking for thomething at the top."

"Well, everything's been shuffled now so..." Roger said.

"Isn't this our song?" Frances asked William.

William blinked as he realized that the couple in the video was him and Frances. They had changed a lot since their freshman year.

In the video, William was awkwardly trying to hold Frances. He looked a complete mess with his hair drenched in sweat. Frances, on the other hand, seemed at ease as she took a second every now and again to try and tuck wispy hairs behind her ears.

The camera swept over them and moved to some other couples dancing.

"Your hair was real long," Roger said to Frances.

"Yeah," Frances whispered, "I might grow it out again."

William stared at Frances for a while, and a smile briefly passed his face.

The video continued for some while until a boy walked in front of the camera.

"Izzy," he started.

"Richard, I'm busy filming for the school," Isabel hissed from behind the camera.

"I know where your besties went," Richard said.

"What?" Isabel asked as the camera moved and scanned the gym room, "Where did they go?"

"Follow me."

Richard led her through the school to the pool room. "They're in there."

"What are they-"

"Shush!" Richard hushed.

The camera lifted to see through the glass window in the door.

"I really like you," William said in a muffled voice from behind the door, "and I've never really liked anyone like thith before."

"I guess this is because I'm a senator's daughter," Frances mumbled.

"No," William reassured her, "My family doeth not vote for hith party."

"Well, neither do I and the rest of the state, but I'm pretty sure a lot of voter fraud is going on.

William began to draw figure eights around the back of his neck. "I know I invited you to the danthe ath a friend, but would you want to go on a date nectht week ath... more than friendth?"

"Really?" Frances asked.

"Really. I love hanging out with you and hearing your theorieth to the point that I look forward to hithtory clath everyday jutht to thee you."

Frances moved closer to him in the video.

"Could I kith you?" William asked.

Slowly, Frances nodded, and William shakily put both hands to her face and pressed an awkward kiss to her lips.

Suddenly, Richard swung the pool door open. "Hey!"

William and Frances were both caught off-guard before William took a faulty step backwards and fell into the pool. At the same time, he accidentally dragged Frances down with him. As they reemerged, Richard was howling with laughter while Isabel was trying to rebuke him.

"Richard, what is wrong with you?" Isabel yelled.

"I'm gonna kill you!" William threatened, as he got out of the pool and ran after Richard, who fled the scene.

"You're so awkward," Roger joked, as he turned around to face William.

William chuckled a little dryly but was surprisingly in good humor. He saw Nina begin to smile before she stared down at her lap.

"What is Richard up to now?" Isabel asked, as she turned to William.

"He'th in jail," William enunciated, "for trying to rob a gath thtathion."

"Oh yikes," Isabel whispered.

"Yeah, he wath awful."

"So, it's easier to pin the pool crime on him?" Frances asked.

"That wath all hith fault," William replied.

His darting eyes landed on the cat. Bear made his way to the front door before passing right through it. The cat had fazed through the door.

Furrowing his brows, William frowned and opened a drawer in the kitchen. He pulled out a flashlight and grabbed his baseball cap.

Frances climbed to her feet and approached him. "Hey, do you want to get anything before we go into the ship? Or do you not want to...?"

"I don't know. I'll trutht your judgement- lithten, I'll be right back, okay?" he said, his attention elsewhere.

"Okay..." she said, looking suspiciously at him.

William took her hand and pressed a kiss to her thumb before moving for the door and stepping out into the dark night to pursue the cat.

Turning the flashlight on, William moved the light about until it landed on the cat who was venturing into the woods. Timbers' woods were dangerous, especially at night. Wolves roamed in there and although they were beginning to learn that their place was deep within, that did not stop some of them from testing the boundaries and making their way into the camp.

With a sigh, William followed the cat, and soon he found himself deep within the woods. The trees seemed larger yet everything looked the same from every direction. This was not the first time William had found himself deep inside the trees and he was certainly not lost, but he was still feeling a sense of great discomfort.

Bear stopped near a small lake before turning around and staring at William. Suddenly, the cat began to scream and as it ran its claws up and down William's leg, it tore at his jeans.

Furrowing his brows, William grew angry and moved his leg in an attempt to get the cat to leave him be. It occurred to him, however, that something was very wrong. Bear seemed desperate, not to mention alarmed.

"Hey," a voice said.

William turned around and pointed his flashlight directly in Roger's face.

"I surrender!" Roger yelled, as he threw his hands in the air.

"What are you doing?" William asked.

"Following you. Frances was kinda concerned when you left."

William frowned, as he stared down at the forest floor. He had not meant to worry Frances.

"What are you doing out here?" Roger asked.

"I wath following the cat."

Roger looked down at the Maine Coon which slowly opened its mouth to reveal a large, terrifying smile. Out of discomfort, Roger cussed.

"What's wrong with the cat?" he inquired.

William took in a deep breath before shrugging loosely.

"Can you come back now?" Roger asked.

"I jutht need thome freth air. I've had a lot on my mind lately."

The two were quiet.

"Why were you so down that one day?" Roger asked.

William blinked. "What?"

"The day with the brownies. You stuck your head inside of your locker and just looked downright miserable. What happened then?"

"I wath jutht upthet. A lot wath going on."

"What was it? If you don't mind me prying."

William could be honest. He knew he could. Still, it felt difficult trying to say the truth.

"I might be Thalatha'th thon," William said.

Roger's eyes widened. "What?"

"I'm her kid..." William repeated.

Staggering backward, Roger gulped. "This is a trap, isn't it?"

William huffed. "I've only been conthidering the pothibility for the latht two weekth."

"So, you're not working for your... mother?"

Shaking his head, William looked away from Roger and fiddled with the flashlight.

Roger cursed softly under his breath. "That's gotta be rough."

"Yeah."

"You could talk to her- stop her-"

"You think the careth what I have to thay?" William yelled.

Roger fell quiet.

"Thalatha wanth nothing more than for me to die," William said.

"Caw!"

The sound caught the two off-guard.

William moved the flashlight around until it landed on a bird. It was one of the *crows*.

"What?" Roger breathed.

"Caw, caw!"

Moving the light, William saw that there was another *bird* right next to the first. He continued to move the flashlight to the right as he found more *birds*. Three. Four. Five.

"Six, seven," Roger counted.

Eight.

Nine.

It kept going. They were surrounded by *kreshlings*.

Ten.

Eleven.

Twelve.

The light landed on an enormous *bird*. No. A man. Poised on a branch among all of the other *crows* was Nagelfar with his large wings fully extended. He was crouching on the branch and leering over the two teenagers.

Thirteen. Thirteen *crows*.

With a loud squawking battle cry, Nagelfar stood tall on the branch.

In the next second, Nagelfar swooped down on his prey and kicked William in the chest with his boots. The force pushed William back, and he was shoved into the lake.

As William tried to get out, he felt hands wrap around his neck and push him further under.

Chapter 23

Thrashing violently, William tried to emerge out of the water, but Nagelfar shoved him further down.

William's head hit the back of a rock, and he watched as blood flowed up amongst the bubbles of his escaping breath.

Pain.

The pain was terrible. There was no escape.

William could feel his lungs threatening to burst. He needed air, and he needed it fast, else he would die in only a matter of time.

Not like this. He could not die like this.

Grabbing at Nagelfar's hands, William tried to free himself desperately. His strength failed him, and he slowly felt himself go limp. He could not fight. Nevermind that he did not have the strength, he did not have the will to fight.

He could hear distorted screaming and shouting outside of the water, but his vision had left him and in the already dark night, nothing could be seen.

The hands released him, yet William stayed under the water. His lungs screamed in pain and pleaded for air. He would die soon if he stayed.

A strange and sudden burst brought his strength back, and William emerged from the water. He gasped, taking in long and deep breaths of air.

He was hyperventilating yet still greatly relieved to breathe again. As William looked around, he searched for Roger and

Nagelfar. He could see the light of the half moon shining through the forest leaves, but it was not illuminating any person besides himself.

They were gone.

Climbing out of the lake, William took in long, deep breaths and padded around on the ground as he looked for the flashlight in the dark.

"Roger?" he called out, "Roger." He had to find him. He had to find Roger.

"You're alive?" a voice asked.

William gripped the flashlight and turned it on. He shined the light in the direction of the voice.

It was Bear.

Shaking from the cold and shock, William nodded.

"I thought he would have killed you," the cat said, as it swished its tail back and forth.

William shook his head.

He had no idea why he was alive. Nagelfar had been intent on killing him and yet the job had been left unfinished. William realized that his jaw was hanging open, but he made no effort to shut it.

"Roger..." he said, as he rubbed the front of his neck. It hurt.

"The boy is gone," Bear whispered.

William felt himself stop breathing again. "What?"

"Nagelfar took him. Flew away."

"No. No..."

The cat stared at him with its bright orange eyes. It was not smiling. It just stared.

"You couldn't have-" William began.

"Are you asking a mere cat?" Bear said with a truly awful smile.

"What do I do?" William asked. His cap and hair were drenched, and a curly lock hung hopelessly out of the baseball hat and dangled in front of his glasses.

"What do you do, William?"

Staring at the ground, William got to his feet as fast as possible before turning around and running back to the house. His lungs were on fire. Not a literal fire though, but it was painful enough. Still, he sprinted as fast as his legs would let him.

Reaching the house, William opened the door and fell forward onto the floor.

"Bill!" Isabel yelled.

Still breathing erratically, William pushed himself up and stared at the four.

"Roger," he said, as he tried to catch his breath.

"What happened?" Frances yelled.

"Why are you wet?" Philip aked.

"Nagelfar," William puffed, "Roger."

His head pounded violently. He could barely even think straight.

"What about Roger?" Philip asked. He had seemed worried before but now he looked panicked.

"Nagelfar took him," William said, as he tried to stand. His legs felt weak, and his head was pounding.

"What?" Frances cried.

Nina's eyes widened, and she began to look around the group.

"Where?" Isabel asked.

"I don't know. Probably the thip," William said.

"The ship never moved," Philip said.

"What?" William asked.

"Thalassa's ship. It never moved. It's still in D.C. as always. Whatever ship Nina fell from wasn't the same one."

"What are you talking about?"

"It's not the same ship, Bill."

"Could it be Nagelfar's?" Frances asked.

"I'd assume," Philip replied, "but we don't know where we'd be going. It's a different ship so Bill wouldn't know what the interior of the ship would look like and what he would need to be imagining to teleport to."

"So, no one knows what the inside of Nagelfar's ship looks like?" Isabel asked.

"I don't know who Nagelfar is, but the ship I was in was Adonis," Nina piped in.

"Adonis'?" Philip asked, taken aback.

"He helped me get off the ship," she explained.

"Do we athume Roger ith on Adonith' thip?" William asked Philip.

"I don't know if we have any other choice," Philip confided, "Could you teleport somewhere just off description?"

That was a more than difficult task and one that William had not tried to accomplish yet. The transports at the hospital could do it, but that took years and years of practice, and William had only been teleporting for about three months now.

He shook his head as he knew it was impossible.

"Wait- that's it!" Isabel exclaimed. She grabbed Nina's hand and dragged her over to Kate's small desk. Isabel started to rifle through William's mother's things.

"You're sure Nagelfar took Roger?" Philip asked.

William shook his head. "Nagelfar had me under water, but they were both gone when I emerged."

"What do you mean Nagelfar had you under water?" Frances asked frantically.

"He tried to drown me," William replied before he started to cough and hack.

"What? Bill!" Frances tried to stand up and move towards him.

William continued to cough and hack in an attempt to clear out his lungs. He still felt delirious and just trying to focus on his girlfriend's face felt like a terribly difficult task.

"Do you have something in your..." Frances trailed off before getting to her knees and blindly trying to find William's backpack which was sitting next to the couch. She located the bag and began rummaging through it.

As she pulled things out, William moved closer to her and looked at the array of items. He tried to help her but was unsure what to do.

Frances turned around and reached out for him before trying to put a hand to his hair. She touched the cap.

"Wh- would you take that off? Why are you even wearing that?" she asked.

William squinted at her while his head tried to make sense of everything going on.

"I think I'm done," Nina said.

"Bill!" Isabel yelled.

"What is this?" Philip asked.

Isabel held up a large sheet of paper which featured an intricate drawing. Nina had drawn the interior of Adonis' ship.

William walked over to Isabel and took the picture from her as everyone else gathered around behind him. "Thith ithn't gonna work," he muttered under his breath.

"It might-" Isabel started.

"It won't! Nina, you draw well, but I can't teleport with thith."

She had drawn exceptionally well. The picture was a first-person view from a balcony which overlooked several other landings, dividers, and metal bridges that connected landings together. William could imagine that the entire interior was as steely as Thalassa's own ship and felt just as cold and uninviting.

As he held the drawing closer to his face, he heard the sound of a gasp from behind him. He felt as three hands began to touch him and then someone wrapped their arms around him from behind.

"Woah," Isabel whispered.

"'Woah' what?" William asked, as he lowered the drawing from his face.

They were in Adonis' ship.

Chapter 24

William wondered how late it was. It had to be at least midnight if not later, but he could not be thinking of that at that moment.

He was in Adonis' ship, and it was just as Nina had drawn.

While looking around, William realized that they were not in fact standing on a balcony but overlooking the railing of a suspended walkway. He put a hand to the arms wrapped around his stomach and looked down. It was Frances. Now, as he turned to both of his sides, he realized that everyone had taken a hold of him when he had teleported.

Nina, Isabel, Philip, Frances, and William were all on the ship.

"That was incredible," Philip breathed.

"What are you guyth-" William started. He blinked and stared at Frances as she pulled back from him, when he noticed she was wearing his backpack for some reason.

"Frank-" he began again. His darting eyes moved to his left arm, and William unleashed a slew of curses.

Isabel screamed, and Nina let out a sound of complete and utter disgust. Philip's bulging eyes widened before he grabbed William to help stable him.

William's left hand was entirely green and as Philip pulled William's plaid overshirt off, the two could see that the green skin extended up his entire arm. As William held up his limp and now growing arm, he watched as his pinkie finger melded with his ring, and his middle finger melded with his index.

"What's happening?" Frances asked panickedly.

Looking to the girls, William could see that they were all horrified.

"Am I *reverting*?" he asked, as he turned to Philip.

"Not yet!" Philip said determinedly. As Philip ripped William's plaid shirt, he created a sling for William's arm.

The arm and the combined fingers were all growing at an alarming rate.

"It's gonna be okay," Philip mumbled, fastening the sling around William's arm and right shoulder.

"I have three fingerth!" William yelled.

"Quiet!" Isabel said through gritted teeth, anxiously looking around the ship.

William looked at his arm which was now in the sling. It was horrifically long as if every bone had expanded to become more than twice its size. Without the sling, his fingers had reached the floor and even with the sling, his hand and fingers were long enough to almost reach his knees.

"Ith thith it?" William asked.

"Not on my watch," Philip replied, "We came here to get Roger. We are getting Roger, and we are not going to lose anyone while we do."

William nodded.

"What's gonna happen to him?" Frances asked. Her face was full of terror.

"He'll be fine," Philip reassured her.

"Bill?" Frances called.

William was unsure of what to do about himself, but this was not about him. He needed to focus on Roger. Roger was in danger and came first.

"We have to find Roger," he asserted.

"Bill-" Isabel started.

"No," William interrupted, "Nina, where would Nagelfar have taken him?"

"I don't know," Nina admitted, "I know where my friend is. He might be with her."

"Lead the way," William instructed.

Looking serious, Nina nodded before moving down the walkway. William and Frances followed close behind, with Philip and Isabel making up the back.

Frances slowly reached out and touched William's arm. He watched her eyes widen as she felt the mushy, green skin.

"I'm gonna be fine," he reassured her.

"I trust you," she whispered.

She should not be trusting him. He had no idea whether he would *revert* or not. He knew he should not be saying he would be fine, because he did not know.

Nina looked over the railing, prompting the rest of the group to do the same. Beneath them were several winged people. It was almost impossible to see anything more than their gigantic wings.

A few men and women without wings approached the winged people. The non-winged people began to yell at the winged people and in front of the group's eyes, one of the men set fire to his fist and punched a winged person in the jaw.

The five watched as a fight broke out between the two groups and soon the screaming and yelling and fighting was beginning to draw attention.

"We need to hide," Philip observed.

William looked at the doors to their right as he tried to figure out which door they should use.

"Nina, where do we go?" Philip asked.

Looking around, Nina tried to decide where to go, when a door opened several feet in front of the five. Two *archiecs* filed out of the room. William could tell they were *archiecs* by the fact that one of them had palms which were on fire.

Quickly, William grabbed hold of Frances' arm with his good hand and dragged her into what he hoped was a now vacant room.

It was. With the two men having gone out to aid their fellow *archiecs*, the room was left completely empty. William motioned for the other three to follow him. Nina, Philip, and Isabel carefully slipped past the two yelling *archiecs* and piled into the room.

Trying to stay out of the *archiecs'* line of sight, the five stayed pressed against the wall while the automatic door ever so slowly shut behind them. They were safe inside the room and with that confirmed, William started to look around at their surroundings.

There were two large desks on either side of the room and several lab coats hanging from hooks. Opposite the door was a small staircase.

On each desk were dozens of dozens of vials. There were seven variations of colors: pink, purple, red, yellow, black, green, and orange.

Cautiously, Philip picked up one of the vials and scrutinized it. "What is this?" he asked hollowly.

William watched as Nina frowned and looked at the vials in disgust.

"Thalatha utheth it for tethting," William explained.

"What?" Philip asked in confusion. He looked to William but then he noticed Nina, and it seemed to click. Thalassa had been using the serum on Nina and the other college students. She was experimenting on them at their expense.

"This way," Nina said, as she approached the small staircase and began to descend. Philip and Isabel nervously followed her lead.

William watched after them but turned his attention to Frances. She reached out and touched the desk before reaching for the vials.

"What are you doing?" William started.

"I'm taking the drugs," Frances said, as she swung the backpack off of her shoulder and began to fill it.

"Why?"

"Because if the doctors back on Earth can figure out whatever this is, they might be able to reverse what Thalassa is doing," Frances explained.

William raised an eyebrow at Frances' cleverness. "Ith that why you brought my backpack?" he asked.

"I was sure there would have to be something we could pocket."

He nodded in admiration. "Have I ever told you how brilliant you are?"

"Yeah, but I'd love to hear you say it again."

"You're brilliant," he said.

He began to pick up some vials, but he paused.

'I think my scientists have it down to two minutes.'

'But you can drink this.'

William would make Thalassa eat those words. He grabbed six of each color except for purple and stuck them into his front pants' pocket before dumping all of the rest into his backpack.

Once it was full, he zipped up the backpack, and Frances swung the bag over her shoulder.

"Let me carry it," William protested.

"I've got it," she reassured him.

"Frank-"

"Bill, I'll be safe." She clutched the backpack's strap tightly and made it known to him that if he wanted the backpack, he would have to forcefully take it from her. And that was not something he would ever try with her.

William descended the stairs warily while keeping Frances close behind him but safe. At the end of the stairs was a balcony with another staircase not far away. Nina, Philip, and Isabel were looking over the balcony's railing at what was beneath them, when William and Frances joined in.

Four tubes were directly under the balcony. In three of the tubes, William could see outlines of creatures. They were large and covered in white fur. Their bulbous bodies could barely even fit within the tube.

Thalassa had completely transformed the college students. It had been hideous to see them before, but this was worse. This was so much worse. It was no longer human beings with animalistic features. It was just animals. She had turned them into animals.

William considered it again and decided he was wrong. These were not animals. These were *haveneaks*.

As William looked at the fourth tube, he felt a wave of relief wash over him followed by a wave of complete and utter dread.

"Roger!" Isabel screamed. Philip was already down the staircase and ready to save his best friend in any way possible. William was next to hit the stairs and as Philip tried to yell through the glass and wake up Roger, William stared in disbelief.

His wandering eyes moved over to a machine that was hooked up to the tube. While there were pink vials attached to the other machines, this vial was green. It made William worried.

Suddenly, Philip began to slam his fists against the glass tube. "Roger!"

As William backed up, Isabel came over, leading Frances along. The girl with the one blue and one green eye could only watch in horror, while her boyfriend pounded against the glass.

"Suey," a voice breathed.

William turned around to see Nina staring at one of the creatures in the other tubes. His eyes darted from the creature to Nina.

"Help me get her out," Nina said, as she turned to William.

William shook his head.

"You have to!" she argued

"Nina, the'th not there!" William shouted, "Whoever the wath, the ithn't that perthon anymore-"

"Philip!" Isabel pleaded.

NOT QUITE BROKEN, NOT QUITE PERFECT

William and Nina turned around to see Philip take a running start before ramming his arm into the tube. Although nothing happened to the tube, Philip looked a little bruised.

In anger, William's brows furrowed. He moved towards Roger's tube and slammed his right fist onto a button.

The water began to drain.

Roger's eyes popped open, and he began to scream, which in turn caused everyone else on the opposite side of the glass to scream as well. Trying to collect his bearings, Roger looked around himself, but he only seemed to be becoming more alarmed by the second.

"Get me out of here!" he yelled.

Philip slapped his hand against the glass. "What do you think we've been trying to do?"

Roger began to hyperventilate inside of the tube as he pounded on the glass.

"There has to be a button. If they put him in there, there has to be a way to get him out," Philip reflected, as he looked around the machines hooked up to the tube.

William's attention was on Roger, however. Roger had his hands pressed on the glass and as he pushed against it, the glass began to vibrate.

Taking hold of Philip, William pulled him away from the tube, as it vibrated faster and faster.

In terror, Roger's eyes widened, and the glass shattered into a million pieces. Isabel screamed before Roger fell face forward out of the tube.

William and Philip both dashed towards Roger and caught him before he could face plant into the shattered glass. Roger was shaking violently.

"What happened?" Roger whispered, as his voice wavered. His attention turned to William, and his mouth fell open ever so slightly. "You're alive…"

Raising an eyebrow, William nodded his head.

Roger put a hand to William's face. "Speak."

"What'th wrong with you!" William yelled.

It was only at that moment that Roger caught sight of William's arm. "What on earth?" Roger screeched at the top of his lungs.

William let go of Roger, but Philip still clung tightly to him.

"What happened?" Roger screamed, "What did you do?"

"Roger," Isabel started.

"What-…" he stuttered, helplessly.

William's eyes darted around the room as he searched for something else to look at. His gaze landed on a weapon sitting on top of one of the many machines.

"What happened?" Philip asked.

"Uh… Nagelfar attacked Bill, and I tried to pry Nagelfar off before he grabbed me. He flew to the ship, and I got dragged into this room. There were some *archiecs* messing around with the machines before I was thrown into the tube. Man, I can't see anything," Roger reflected, as he pulled off his glasses.

His clothes were soaking wet, but William was unsure if he was shaking from adrenaline or from being submerged under ice cold water. It had to have been adrenaline that broke the glass. William's eyes glanced at the green vial.

It had to be adrenaline.

The sound of yelling drew the six's attention to the staircase where the two *archiecs* from before were standing. The *archiecs* were screaming something in French, but William did not even bother to take a moment to translate any of it.

As one of the *archiecs* reached for his weapon, William grabbed the weapon that was sitting on the machine and fired at the two. His aim was significantly off, especially since he was using his right hand, but both *archiecs* appeared to be scared as the *archiec* no longer bothered to try and grab his gun.

"Geler!" William yelled.

'Freeze.'

The two froze.

William turned to Philip, all while the gun was still trained on the two. "What do we do?"

Philip looked surprised. "Wait, you're asking me?"

"What do we do, Philip," William repeated.

"... we escape?" Philip suggested.

"How?" William yelled, becoming annoyed.

"We could teleport if you weren't in *reversion* but because you are, there's no guaranteeing you could get us all to the ground. Plus, we don't even know how far we are into the air right now," Philip explained.

The *archiecs* slowly backed away before William fired another warning shot.

"Nan," William said.

'Nope.'

"Cosse!" Isabel yelled to the *archiecs*.

'Pod.'

"What?" William asked.

"If we can't teleport away, we could use a space pod, right? They have to have space pods," she argued, "Où sont les gousses espace?"

'Where are the space pods.'

The *archiecs* began talking amongst each other, when William closed one eye and tried to aim for one of their heads. The two exchanged a quick glance before beginning to talk.

"Le troisième niveau. Porte quinze," one of them said.

'Third level. Gate fifteen.'

"Je vous remercie," Isabel said, delighted.

'Thank you.'

Confused, the *archiecs* looked to one another.

"French really does pay off," Isabel reflected.

"What level are we now?" William asked.

"Five if I'm right," Roger mumbled.

"He's right," Nina affirmed quietly.

"This is awful. Literally everything hurts," Roger said, as he closed his eyes tightly in pain. He opened his eyes and looked to Nina. "Oh hey. You came too."

Nina raised both of her eyebrows at him but nodded. Taking one final look at her friend, Nina pulled her gaze away and approached Philip to help aid Roger. Roger's knees were shaking, and it looked as if he might collapse at any second.

"Thanks for helping out," Roger said.

"Well, it would seem that I'm stuck with the five of you, so I might as well," she muttered.

"Morgan, help Frank out," William ordered.

With his weapon still on the *archiecs*, William carefully moved toward the enemy. He kept the gun trained on the *archiecs*, as the six passed.

Once outside of the room, William looked around. He was unsure of where to go next.

"How do we get to the third level?" he asked, as he turned to Nina.

The sound of yelling echoed from below. Roger tried to take a peek over the railing and pulled Nina and Philip along with him.

"I can say for certain that the first level is covered in fire," Roger announced.

The other three peered over, and it was just as awful of a mess as they could imagine. There were bodies lying everywhere, and the fighting only continued. *Kreshlings* were clawing out *archiecs'* eyes, and *archiecs* were setting *kreshlings* on fire.

It was war. They had turned on one another.

William watched as Nagelfar entered the scene and began yelling something in Spanish. Another man followed close behind him, and the two tried to break up the fighting.

Staring down, William focused on the second man. He was wearing a red tabard and his head had limited gray hair to show since he was balding.

The man looked up.

Although the first level was miles below the fifth, it appeared as if the man's eyes were widening behind his spectacles at the sight of the six.

"Move," William barked. The six backed up from the railing and started to move around the landing to find a way to get to the third level.

A glowing green outline appeared ten feet ahead of them, and it slowly became more vibrant as the man materialized in front of their eyes.

The six stopped dead in their tracks.

It was Adonis.

Adonis started at the six teenagers. William was fully prepared to set Adonis on fire at any second, but something made him hesitate.

As Adonis looked over the group, he paused, and his eyes widened. "Nina?"

"Adonis," she replied.

"She's with the enemy..." Roger mumbled. William furrowed his brows.

"The enemy?" Adonis asked, looking completely bewildered, "What are you talking about?"

"You're conspiring with Thalassa!" Isabel yelled.

"I am not!" Adonis yelled.

"You're housing her tests on your ship," Frances reminded him.

"She commandeered my ship," Adonis explained.

"Listen, he's not an enemy! He helped get me off of this ship," Nina argued in his defense.

"He hasn't helped the rest of Earth," Frances said, looking angry.

"I do not have the power to do that," Adonis said.

"You could still try, man," Roger piped in.

"Do you have any idea the decisions I have to make as a guardian?" Adonis asked.

"Decisions like making peace treaties with every galaxy which has resulted in the *nebulan* race being oppressed by all other *alien* races?" Philip retorted.

Adonis opened his mouth before closing it. "Now, listen here, young man."

"I'm listening," Philip replied.

William was impressed by Philip's aggressiveness. He was certainly showing Adonis what for.

"I have established peace. I have not gone out and sought war like many of my fellow guardians. I have made my planet a safe haven," Adonis explained.

"You've made a knockoff version of Haven," Philip spat, "Just more dangerous."

"Are you a *nebulan*, son?"

"*Quiznic*."

"Then, shut your mouth. I am not going to kill any of you kids."

"Awesome. We'll be going," Roger said, nudging Philip furiously.

"Now, hold on for one second. I have a few questions for all of you. What are you doing here? And who are all of you children to be snooping around on a guardian's ship?" Adonis turned to Nina, "And why are you back here? I snuck you off to save you, not so that you would return with your posse!"

"Why not the other kidth?" William asked.

"Yeah! You left all of the other students," Frances yelled.

"As terrible as what Thalassa is doing, at least the other children were taking to her testing and had strong vitals. Nina was completely failing. The tests were making her worse, she was losing weight at an alarming rate, and Thalassa was only considering her as nothing more than a fluke. An outlier to her tests," Adonis explained.

"I removed her because Thalassa had practically fried her. I never expected her to come back," he finished.

"She came back because our friend got abducted," Frances explained, as she tried to point at Roger. She looked beyond mad.

William lifted her arm a little so that she could point to the right person.

"What 'abducted?'" Adonis repeated, "Al does not-"Thalassa does not abduct people."

"Huh. There are three people still in tubes who might argue otherwise," Frances quipped.

"It is terrible what she has done, but those three snuck onto the ship to begin with, and Thalassa considered that to be fair play. She does not go out of her way to abduct people."

"We were still taken against our will," Nina said, growing upset.

"And that was terrible, but Thalassa does not abduct people."

"No, but Nagelfar apparently does," Frances said.

Adonis paused. "Nagelfar did what?"

"He abducted me after trying to drown my friend here," Roger said, as he motioned to William, "Is that a good enough explanation for why we're here and who we are?"

As William looked up, he made eye contact with Adonis. Adonis' eyes widened, and his mouth fell slightly ajar while he stared at William. William wanted to be anywhere else, but his feet were stuck to the floor, and his entire body was frozen.

The other five looked between the guardian and William in confusion.

Adonis approached William when Isabel, Frances, Roger, and Philip formed a wall between the two. William looked to his group before looking to Adonis. He was almost surprised to see everyone being protective of him.

"You were on Thalassa's ship. You were the one who released that video," Adonis said.

William raised a brow. "Ith that all?" he asked. He was hoping that was all.

Adonis was silent. "Llacheu?" he whispered.

Roger looked to Frances and as Isabel looked to Philip, Philip turned to William. Philip's eyes were as wide as saucers.

William kept his gaze trained on Adonis as he nodded.

The old man pushed past the other teenagers before standing directly in front of William. "It really is you?"

William had to come to terms. There was nothing left for him to do. He nodded defeatedly, letting his wandering eyes try to find something else to look at.

"You've been working against us?" Philip asked.

"He only found out a few weeks ago," Roger said, elbowing Philip.

Adonis grabbed hold of William and hugged him tightly. William was alarmed, but he had no idea how to fight off the hug.

"I thought you were dead," Adonis whispered, "She told me you were dead. I thought you were long gone. I thought you died years ago."

William was unsure exactly how to react.

"And then I see you on the ship, and I am told I am just going crazy. Llacheu!" Adonis held William at an arm's length away and looked at him before noticing the glaring issue: William's arm.

"What?" Adonis started.

"The arm?" Roger asked.

"Thalassa got rid of the *nikolates*," Frances piped up, "Probably."

"I know... I could not stop her," Adonis said quietly before turning his attention back to William, "I have been trying to find you this last month, and then Thalassa boarded my ship, and I had to put my work on hold to keep you safe-"

"Well, the obviouthly found your work becauthe the thent *quithnicth* and Nagelfar after me," William replied.

Adonis frowned. "I am sorry."

William considered shrugging, but it did not seem appropriate at that moment. His brows furrowed as the gears turned in his head, and something else occurred to him. "Thalatha ith on your thip."

"She commandeered it, yes," Adonis started.

"The commandeered the thip of another powerful guardian, and he wathn't able to fight back?"

Adonis opened his mouth before closing it. "I am not really in a position to fight back-"

"Tho, you'd rather aid her?"

"Adonis!" a voice shouted.

The six and Adonis peered over the railing. William watched as Nagelfar screamed from the first level. Nagelfar was throwing a fit and kicking lifeless bodies.

"Go," William instructed the group.

Philip met William's eyes and looked hesitant yet he complied. Pulling Roger, Philip passed Adonis, and the rest of the group followed.

"I can help," Adonis offered.

"I don't trutht you," William replied bluntly.

"What have I done-"

"You're aiding the enemy!"

"I am not! I am just without the resources to fight back-"

"Whith ith why you've keeled over and let her and Nagelfar thtathion *archiecth* and *krethlingth* on your thip?"

Adonis struggled to get the words out.

"The obviouthly hath acthetht to the *quithnic* and *krethling* army. Doeth the have actheth to the *nebulan* army too?" William questioned.

Adonis looked away, as he appeared to be growing uncomfortable.

"Were you aiding her to find me?"

There was no response.

William frowned bitterly and pushed past Adonis.

"I am sorry..." Adonis said softly behind him.

William did not bother to reply. He caught up with the rest of the group and tried to push Adonis as far from his mind as possible.

"Keep moving," William ordered.

The six approached a set of stairs and descended into the fourth level. Once they reached level four, the stairs ended.

"We're on level four, I think," Roger slurred, as he stared at a blatant sign reading 'L4.'

Annoyed, William glared down at Roger. However, his glare softened almost immediately. Roger did not look well at all.

"The other flight of stairs is on that side," Nina said, as she pointed to the opposite end of the level.

As William looked over the landing, the sounds of more yelling and screaming hit his ears. He thought that the fighting on level one had ended, but it seemed to be getting worse now.

"We need to get to the pods," Isabel urged.

Philip nodded. "Come on, guys."

William raised an eyebrow. He and Philip both knew who was the leader, but William was willing to hand the mantle over to Philip while William was stuck in his current condition.

Nina started down the hallway. Surprised, Philip and William exchanged a glance before following her lead. The group walked the length of the hallway with bated breath. Everyone knew that one faulty move, one door opening, one angry *kreshling* flying up from the first floor to at least the fourth could mean the end of all of their lives.

Looking around, William could not focus on any one thing. His eyes had to dart from one place to another. It was one way he could keep everyone safe.

Aggressively, William fiddled with his weapon. He managed to find a way to attach it to one of the belt loops on his jeans, and that brought him a little bit of peace. At the very least, it was something he could no longer unthinkingly mess around with.

He turned to his right and saw an open door. The door was not what drew his attention though. While it was alarming to see an open door, it was more alarming to see what was inside of the room.

There was a desk with an orb on top of it. Behind the desk, there were numerous shelves, but William was not paying attention to any of those details. He was paying attention to the cat sitting in front of the desk.

It was Bear.

William was most uncomfortable by the fact that the Maine Coon was not smiling. It just stared at him. Just stared.

William stopped walking and stared inside.

Isabel looked behind her shoulder and took notice of him before bringing herself and Frances to a stop. "Bill?" she called out in confusion.

"Gimme a thecond," he said.

"What? What are you doing?" Frances asked, growing alarmed.

"Hey, maybe don't," Philip started to argue.

"Dude! Number one rule: don't split up. That's how people die," Roger yelled.

"Can we please just stick to the objective at hand and get to the pods?" Nina pleaded.

"No- all of you, jutht thut up!" William yelled, "Gimme one thecond, alright?" He furrowed his brows and turned to look at the terrible cat.

As he entered the room, the door slid shut behind him. The rest of the group yelled and shouted and called his name, while William whirled around and watched in complete disbelief as the door closed.

"Am I supposed to be impressed?" a voice asked.

Turning again, William looked up to see Thalassa standing at the top of a staircase.

"Well? Am I supposed to be impressed?" she repeated.

He shrugged. "Well, thure."

She seemed even less impressed by that statement. She scowled down at him, and William felt his heart stop. The daggers she was throwing with her eyes alone should have been enough to kill him.

"You always have to... to... get in the way, do you not?" Thalassa hissed. She began to descend the stairs.

William's eyes darted to the cat which moved away and around the side of the desk furthest from Thalassa.

"I get in the way?" William asked.

Thalassa paused in her descent and gripped the railing tightly. "I would have thought that was obvious when I removed the *nikolates*."

Looking to his arm, William stared at the green, mushy skin. He bet that Thalassa was pretty proud of herself.

"I hoped you might be your own undoing yet here you are with your posse," Thalassa observed.

"'My pothe?'" William struggled to ask.

"I have been watching you and your little friends run around the ship. Adonis tapped into my security cameras so I figured I might tap into his."

"You don't like people mething with your thtuff, but you theem fine mething with their'th. Theemth a little hypocritical."

"People should already realize that I am above them. I am of higher standing."

William tried to back up as Thalassa finally stepped off of the stairs.

"I would not move anymore if I were you," Thalassa advised.

"What do you want from me?" William asked.

"You know, strangely enough, I was wondering the exact same thing about you. You sneak onto my ship, you take videos and release them to the world, you sneak on again just to watch me and Nagelfar. What do you want, Llacheu?"

The name made him uncomfortable.

"I am your thon, aren't I?" William asked.

"I wish you were not," Thalassa hissed, "You are the spitting image of your father at his age. Curly hair, thick eyebrows, tanned skin, same height, same build, same everything. The only difference is that at least your father smiled."

Thalassa came inches away from William's face. "Let me see that smile."

William's eyes darted from her syrupy cognac eyes to the large ring dangling on the end of her necklace. He wondered if it was Caracy's ring.

"I should gouge out your eyes. They do not belong to you," Thalassa said, as she stared intently at him.

His cognac eyes locked back with her's.

"I should spill your blood too while I am at it, so I can ensure you have nothing of mine," she said, while walking towards the desk, "however, I would rather not spill any more blood tonight."

"You haven't thpilled any yet. I'm thtill alive."

Thalassa stared at him quizzically. "Whatever are you on about?"

"Your drowning plan didn't work."

"My 'drowning plan?'" she repeated.

"You thent Nagelfar to drown me in a lake."

This was obviously news to her. "I did not send him to do any such thing."

"Well, it thure theemth like you run a tight thip."

She looked mad but not necessarily at him. "It seems like all of the *kreshlings* need to be put in their rightful place."

"They don't apprethiate you? That'th thurprithing."

Thalassa glared at him. "Sometimes they work up the nerve to question my authority. So, I like to try and send a few of my men their way."

"The mathacre down on the firtht level?" William assumed.

"I do not know if I would call it a massacre."

"Thothe are all your men: both the *archiecth* and the *krethlingth*."

"'Those.'" She said, "It is 'those,' Llacheu. Is it so hard for you to pronounce a simple 's?'"

Glaring, William considered how much he would like to hold his tongue. He figured not at all. As he opened his mouth to spit a few choice words at her face, she cut him off.

"I want to strike a deal with you," she explained.

William furrowed his brows. He was unconvinced. "Uh huh?"

Calmly, she rested her hands on the desk for a moment. "I think you could be of some use to me, William, and that is the only reason you are not dead just yet."

William's glare faltered. Thalassa had called him by the name Kate had given him, and he found that alarming. Although he knew she was aware of his name and that Mr. Homfry had introduced him by that name to her so long ago, the name still sounded disgusting coming out of her mouth.

"What uthe could I pothibly be to you?" William asked.

"Llacheu, whether of course you believe it or not, you are not quite useless," she explained, "Not quite broken."

"Not quite perfect, but gueth the thame goeth for you," he replied.

Thalassa glared at him.

"Do you think you're a god or thomething?" William questioned.

"What do you believe-"

"I believe in God, the Three in One-"

"What do you believe is going to come out of you making little jabs at me?" she barked.

"I'll tick you off enough for you to kill me?"

Thalassa stared at him and although she might have believed she was leaving the question unanswered, it was answer enough for William.

"I want you to *revert* for me," Thalassa explained.

William felt his heart skip a beat as he raised a brow. "You want me to *revert*?"

"You run around Haven for a short while, and then I will save your planet from the destruction you unleashed and could further unleash."

Angrily, William gritted his teeth before snarling at Thalassa.

"In return, I will compensate you."

"'Compenthate me?'" William repeated.

"I will provide you a home. A place for you, the senator's daughter- Frances, was it?" Thalassa asked, "And that... Kate Mason."

His breathing stopped completely.

"And every now and again, I will pull you out to do a little favor for me. What do you say to that?"

"No."

"'No?'"

"You can't harm my planet."

"I am to believe you care about it?"

"Why wouldn't I?"

"Well, it would seem that you never really have. You were expelled from your middle school, you have been suspended from your high school before, and it seems you are en route to being suspended again."

"Now, how would you know that?"

"You do not seem to be appreciated much by anyone."

"That'th enough," William growled.

"What has the world ever done for you? Why would you bother trying to save Haven?"

"Becauthe I'll never have peathe, if you take the planet my family loveth away from them. I'll never forgive mythelf, if I could have kept them from being torn apart and didn't do a thing, and I would never have my retht."

"How sentimental."

"You can mock me ath muth ath you like but at leatht, I care about thomeone."

Thalassa glared at him and sent daggers his way. However, her glare lightened. Only slightly though. "You are amusing," she commended.

William did not like that.

Suddenly, Bear jumped up on the table and turned his face and horrific smile to Thalassa. The guardian's attention snapped to the cat.

"Hello there," she greeted.

William looked between the cat and the guardian. "Are you familiar with him?"

"I do not believe that is any of your business," Thalassa confided.

"It'th my girlfriend'th cat. It'th all of my buthineth."

"Oh is it now?" she asked. Her gaze remained trained on the Maine Coon.

She picked up the orb on the table and smashed the cat's head in with it. She smashed it again and again and again and yelled while she did it.

William's brows rose in horror as he watched.

Finally, she stopped and set the orb back down before gracefully moving to the staircase as if nothing had happened.

Frances.

That was all William could think about: Frances. She would be crushed. Nevermind how much he hated the cat. Nevermind how disgusting and terrifying it was. It was still Frances' cat.

"Thalatha!" William yelled, while she ascended the stairs. He approached the desk and looked at what was left of the cat's head. There was blood everywhere, and the only thing he could manage to do was pick up the lifeless cat and cradle it in his one good arm.

He could not even begin to think of how Frances would react.

"Thalatha!" William shouted again. He set the cat down and removed his weapon from his belt loop before taking aim. He intended to kill Thalassa but his aim was so off, he only hit her in the arm.

Still, an arm for an arm.

Thalassa shrieked and looked at the damage. She gripped her now bloody arm and set her gaze on William. "You little-!"

Immediately, William knew he needed to leave. He reattached the weapon to the belt loop, scooped up the dead cat, and imagined the outside of the door.

Chapter 26

William teleported to see the five he had left behind still yelling and hammering on the door.

"What are you doing!" William shouted.

The five turned around. Everyone was staring at William before they looked at the dead and mangled cat in William's arm. Everyone except Frances.

Roger's eyes widened, and the two boys stared at each other. This was not the time. There would never be a time.

"Go! Run!" William yelled.

The group broke into a mad dash for the stairs. As he ran, William was struggling to hold the cat. He looked to his right arm to see green splotches slowly appear. Turning his attention back to the cat, William suddenly noticed it was gone. It had fazed out of existence.

"What..." he breathed.

Philip turned around. "Where did the cat go?"

William shook his head in confusion. He had no idea.

"What cat?" Frances asked, as she stopped moving.

"We need to keep going," William said, trying to push her along.

"What cat, Bill? My cat?" she yelled.

William grabbed hold of her arm and forcefully pulled her. He did not want to be so forceful with her, but he had no choice.

"Bill- let me go!"

"Honey, pleathe. Jutht trutht me right now!" he begged.

She shut up and started to move along with him but was mumbling under her breath to him. She was begging him for answers, but William could not provide her any. He was trying to keep her safe as he could, but he still pulled her down the stairs as quickly as he could manage, while the six descended into the third level.

Frances had begun to cry which caused William more distress, but he could barely hear her sobs as one voice rang out louder than all the rest.

"Layton!" Thalassa screamed.

William looked up before cursing.

"We're too late," Roger wheezed.

"Not yet!" William yelled.

"We're here!" Nina cried.

They had reached the pods. Philip handed Roger over to Nina and kicked one of the pods as forcefully as he could in an attempt to open the hatch.

"Layton!" Thalassa cried. The six looked up to see her leaning over the railing. She was still clutching her bleeding arm. "Layton! Layton!"

"Thalassa," Nagelfar said, as he landed next to her on the railing. His wings were spread out as he sat perched.

"Did I call you?" Thalassa asked.

"No, but I-"

"You are getting on my nerves, Nagelfar."

"I just tried-"

"You were not to drown him. If I want to kill him, I will do it myself!" Thalassa pulled her hand away from her arm before setting her palm on fire. In an instance, she put her hand on Nagelfar's face.

His screams were muffled and as he tried to pull her hand away, he only burned himself more. Thalassa removed her hand and all that could be seen of Nagelfar's face was a bloody and charred mess.

The guardian fell backwards off of the railing and plummeted down four levels. Isabel screamed as the winged man hit the floor. If he was not dead before, he was dead now.

William looked over the railing. It was horrifying. The man was a complete bloody mess, and it was obvious he would not be getting back up again. The *kreshlings* began to scream and howl as they beheld the scene. They stared at the corpse of their guardian.

"Layton!" Thalassa yelled at the top of her lungs while she still awaited the arrival of her supposed savior.

The *kreshings* had fury in their eyes and attempted to fly up to Thalassa. The *archiecs*, however, were not about to let them. With flames in their hands, the *archiecs* grabbed at the *kreshlings'* wings.

Philip opened the pod he was working on. "Come on! Get the other ones open!"

William turned around and aided Philip in opening two more of the pods.

"The pods will only fit one person, so we'll each be taking separate ones," Philip explained, "Look for a symbol of an upside down chair."

"What?" Roger mumbled. He was completely out of it. He did not look good at all.

"Upside down chair. Are you listening?" Philip asked William.

William nodded.

Philip grabbed hold of Isabel and helped her into one of the pods. William followed suit and led Frances into her own pod.

"What happened to my cat?" Frances asked quietly, as William strapped in the safety belt.

"He'th fine," William lied.

"Bill," she whispered. He looked down to meet her eyes and could see tears streaming down her face. "Is Bear gone?"

William blinked and used his right thumb to wipe away the tears from her left cheek. "Hey, hey. It'th all gonna be alright. Bear ith fine."

As William looked at the symbols, he swiped the screen to the left and a new symbol arrived. He continued swiping when he saw a symbol he recognized. He had seen it before somewhere. The gears turned in William's head, and he questioned if he knew the symbol because it had been in his own pod when he was sent to Earth.

His eyes moved to the pod's window, and he could see the half moon outside. It was far away, but it still gave off an illuminating white light.

"You're gonna be okay, Frank," he told her, while turning his eyes back to her.

"Bill," she whimpered.

As he stared at the teary eyed girl, he pressed a kiss to her forehead before pressing a dozen more. "It'th gonna be okay," he told her, "I'll thee you thoon."

"Bill," she cried out.

He was feeling terribly claustrophobic in the small pod, and he could feel his heart threatening to burst out of his chest, but he continued to stare at the terribly sad face.

"Please," Frances begged.

"I love you," he whispered.

William pulled his head out of the cramped pod and sealed the hatch. Pressing the button next to the hatch, he watched as the pod took off. He hoped she would be alright. She would have to be alright.

He turned to his right to see Philip and Nina working on another pod.

"Morgan and Roger?" William asked.

"They're safe," Philip affirmed.

Layton had reached Thalassa and was shouting commands to a group of *quiznics*. As William watched, his brows furrowed. He turned to Philip and Nina who were panickedly trying to pry open a hatch. William's right hand brushed against this pocket, and his brows slowly rose.

He had a dangerous idea.

Chapter 27

William turned to Philip. "I'm making thith end tonight."

"What?" Philip asked.

"Thalatha ithn't gonna thend uth running any longer. I'm ending thith tonight," he asserted.

"We're completely outnumbered," Philip argued, as he let go of the pod's hatch.

"Do you trutht me?"

"Of course not! We can't win a thing like this!"

"Philip!"

"I got it open!" Nina yelled.

"Two minuteth," William pleaded, as he locked eyes with Philip, "Buy me two minuteth time and then you can ethcape with everyone elthe."

Philip looked around as if he was trying to find Isabel to back him up. Isabel was gone though. She was safe.

"What's gonna happen to you?" Philip asked.

"I'll be fine," William said.

"Bill, I can't go back to Isabel without you. She would never forgive me."

"I'll be fine!" William yelled, "Two minuteth! We don't have time to argue over thith!"

Nina looked desperately between the two.

"Go!" William instructed her before turning back to Philip, "You go too. I'll do it mythelf."

"I'll buy you two minutes," Philip resigned, "but you have to escape in a pod too."

William nodded. "I will."

It was a lie. He had no idea if he would make it far enough to escape. William was ready to go down fighting tonight.

Nina closed her hatch and activated the pod from the inside before it shot off.

"Okay," Philip whispered hoarsely, "Okay."

"Thank you," William said.

Philip looked around himself and dashed off to the stairs.

William pulled the vials out of his pocket. He put the red one back in his pocket and stared at the remaining five. He held the five close to his chest with his bad left arm and pulled the lids off of the vials before taking them back in his right hand. Breathing heavily, William swallowed back any fear in his chest and knocked back the serums.

It was a bitter disgusting taste like absolutely no other. The liquids were thick, and they all appeared to be immiscible as none of them were mixing together.

Pain.

It burned his throat and caused William to cough and gag. Making a fist with his right hand, William hammered his chest and tried to make the liquids go down and stay down. He had no idea what he was doing, but he was determined.

He tried to count in his head, but the moment the serums hit his stomach, he felt like he had been punched in the gut, and his mind began to swirl.

Pain.

Dropping the vials, William grabbed hold of the railing as the glass shattered on the floor. His vision was going haywire, and he felt he might throw up at any second.

Pain.

Letting out a cry, William closed his eyes tightly. This was like *reckoning* but a thousand times worse. It felt like every inch of him was being torn apart molecule by molecule. It probably was. His DNA was probably being rewritten and that was what this excruciating pain was.

"Thalassa, stop this!" Adonis shouted.

Through his distorted vision, William watched Adonis approach Thalassa and Layton.

Pain.

William gritted his teeth tightly as he felt a massive burning sensation shoot up and down his arms. He clutched his left arm and pulled off the makeshift sling.

"I have had enough!" Adonis asserted.

"Quiet!" Thalassa yelled before turning to Layton, "I want him found now!"

Layton nodded. Even from the great distance between William and the guardians, William could see how severe Layton looked.

A loud howl erupted, and William watched as the guardians tried to figure out where the noise was coming from. Up on the fifth level, three *havenesks* were peering over the railing and letting out enormous roars.

The *aliens* down on level one stopped their fighting and looked up at the new contenders.

"How did they get out?" Thalassa yelled.

"I'm not sure-" Layton started.

"Shut up!" Thalassa screamed.

Pain.

William held himself tightly as he felt all of the agony consume him. He watched the *havenesks* jump from the fifth level down to the first. Their jump had left them entirely unharmed, and they started to rip into both the *archiecs* and *kreshlings* alike.

"You are going to remove yourself from Haven!" Adonis shouted, loud enough to be heard by every living being on the ship, "You are going to stop this now or so help me, I will declare war, and I will have the *recquads* and *lifrishmics* declare war against you as well."

"Can you not see I am busy?" Thalassa yelled, "I am through with your idle threats."

Pain.

William closed his eyes tightly and bit down on his tongue. He considered for an instance that he might exert enough force as to bite through his tongue.

It was horrendous. He felt like his legs might give out beneath him at any moment as he clutched the railing even tighter.

His eyes were still showing him a distorted world where silver and chrome were green and yellow. It was agonizing to look around.

"They are not idle," Adonis said, "*Neblimsh* declares war against *Archia*."

Guards surrounded Thalassa, and William assumed that they must be *nebulans*.

"Really?" Thalassa asked.

"Really," Adonis affirmed, "Layton, choose what you want now."

Layton looked between the two. It was obvious that he was unsure how to react.

"After all this time," Thalassa yelled, "You scheming, worthless worm!"

Thalassa let go of her arm and flames once again erupted from her hand. Fire spread around her before consuming the *nebulan* guards. Thalassa pulled her sword out of its sheath and ran it through Adonis.

William's brows rose before he shut his eyes tightly, as he was hit with another wave of striking torture.

Pain.

Adonis said something that could not reach William's ears. Everything sounded faded. His ears were only picking up white noise and nothing else.

William could, however, hear Thalassa's screaming reply, and he opened his eyes just in time to see Thalassa push Adonis over the railing.

"Thalassa!" Layton yelled.

"Would you like to be next?" Thalassa screeched.

William looked down at the man and was uncertain how to feel or react. That man was his father. He had no idea what to think.

Turning to his left, William saw another person staring over the railing. After a second, the person turned to him, and the two locked eyes.

"Philip," William breathed.

"Does that buy you two minutes?" Philip yelled, as he ran over to William.

NOT QUITE BROKEN, NOT QUITE PERFECT

William opened his mouth before looking down at the *havenesks*. "I don't know how you did that but yeah, it doeth. Go. Get out of here."

Quiznics were descending down into the third level.

"C'mon!" William yelled. The two ran to a pod and pulled at the hatch until it swung open for them. Quickly, Philip climbed inside.

"Go!" William yelled, as he backed up.

His vision was relaxing, and he could actually see the world as it was again. He stared at the ground and focused as he tried to call out an ability. He had to feel light. He felt so heavy, but he needed to feel light.

He felt tears in his shirt, but then felt two enormous wings sprout from his back and expand to their full wingspan.

Philip's bulging eyes widened. "Bill?"

"I thaid go!" William yelled. He turned around and stared up at the fourth level. His mouth was hanging open slightly. He could not believe it had actually worked. He felt horrible, but it had worked. He was now one more kind of *alien*.

He hated it.

William flapped the wings as he tried to get a feel for the new horrible ability. He put one foot onto the railing, then the other, flapped the wings a few times, and jumped in the hopes that he was not about to kill himself.

The wings pulled him into the air. It felt strange and impossible, but he was flying. Focusing deliberately, he continued to use the wings. His heart was in his stomach, and he did his best to imagine himself not dropping at any moment.

Rising, William flew just above Thalassa and Layton. Thalassa was staring at him in horror.

William smiled slyly. "Hi. Remember me?"

He folded the wings in and fell before kicking Thalassa in the chest. She fell back hard while coughing and trying to collect her bearings.

William set the back of his right hand on fire before throwing a right hook and nailing Layton in the jaw.

Layton cried out and stumbled back.

"I thtill got it," William said in amazement.

Thalassa stood up and set her good hand on fire. She let the flame climb up her arm. The woman had death in her eyes.

William focused on extending himself, and a vine erupted from his right wrist. However, Thalassa quickly set it on fire.

Adrenaline was coursing through William's blood. He had felt this feeling before while boxing but in boxing, his life was not at stake.

Two new arms formed beneath his two other arms and weighed him down. He had no control over his new abilities, and they were all happening at once. He was experiencing every emotion and feeling known to man, and the abilities were all conflicting.

When he had first gone through *reckoning*, he had experienced great difficulty honing just one ability at a time, nevermind two. He had no bearing over five new added abilities.

Breathing heavily, William tried to focus and pull water from the air. He directed the ball of water at Thalassa but she easily evaded it without a problem.

He did not feel well. Something felt very wrong. He looked at his many arms and saw how severe the *reversion* was growing.

"Oh, sweet child. Are you scared?" Thalassa asked.

Looking up, William saw malice in her eyes.

Pain.

He gritted his teeth as he looked down and watched claws erupt from the fingers on his lower hands. His strength was gone. There was nothing left.

Pain.

He could feel his body ripping itself to shreds as it grew heavier with every second.

"Layton, open the hanger," Thalassa instructed.

Layton climbed to his feet, and William saw the damage he had inflicted. A serious and severe burn covered the left side of Layton's face. Extending his hand, Layton let a vine grow before it passed William.

William pressed himself to the left hand wall harder than he had meant to as he tried to avoid the vine. Turning around, he watched the vine touch a part of the wall which slowly opened up. He had not realized how far he had backed up while Thalassa had been advancing towards him.

Pain.

His head was swirling. It hurt so much. He was losing his remaining grip to reality. He felt like his head might crack open at any second. If it did not crack open on its own, he might crack it himself just to make the pain stop.

The half moon and stars were moving rapidly as his vision started to go.

William looked back at his enemy. As she continued to advance, Thalassa pulled back her flames. Breathing heavily,

William looked over the side to see that his only option to evade her was dropping thousands of feet to Earth.

Turning back, William saw that his mother was directly in front of him.

"Thank you," Thalassa whispered.

She began to unsheath her sword before butting the hilt into his chest and knocking the remaining wind out of him.

William lost his footing and fell backwards into the air before everything went black.

Chapter 28

William took in a deep breath as his eyes opened, and he looked around himself. He was lying down in an exam chair in a bright white room.

Several people were surrounding him but backed up as he moved his head around. He was attempting to figure out where he was when the examiners all suddenly started yelling in Russian.

While William tried to process what was going on, he wondered if he was dead.

Covered in sweat, William noticed that his hair was stuck to his face. His brown hair was just as curly as ever, but it appeared to be longer. He wondered how long he had been asleep. Hopefully, he had been asleep.

"Llacheu!" a voice yelled.

William looked ahead of himself to see two blurry figures approaching him.

A woman put something in his hand and after a second, he recognized that it was his glasses.

"Thank you?" he said.

He put on the glasses and saw a lanky man with pale skin and dark brown hair and another man who was much larger. The second man had light brown skin and dark brown hair as well as a lion's mane beard.

"I'm so glad you're okay," the lanky man said as he sat down next to William, "How are you feeling?"

William furrowed his brows as he stared at the man in confusion.

"Gairbith, give him some space!" the second man yelled.

"Right. Sorry," Gairbith said before moving away.

William noticed that the larger man was wearing a green tabard and displaying four arms. This was Cenred.

Cenred stood in front of William and let out a slow breath before putting all four arms on the armrests of William's chair.

"Do you know who I am?" Cenred asked.

"You're Thenred. You're the *recquad* guardian," William said with a frown. He was ready to start a fight although he was well aware that he had no strength at all.

"I am your godfather, appointed by your father, Adonis," Cenred explained.

William raised a brow at him.

"Welcome to *Resuvas*, Llacheu," Cenred said, "There is a lot you have missed."